"I Only Want You,"

Will told Krista.

It required incredible effort not to look away from the determination and longing in his eyes. Being wanted by Will Sutherland was a heady sensation. It always had been. Eight years ago he would have accented a statement like that with a wink or a raised eyebrow. Today, he stared directly into her eyes, waiting for her answer.

The changes in him were as intriguing as the things that were the same. And Krista didn't want to be intrigued by him. Intrigue had a way of leading to heartache. That thought set off a warning inside her head. She'd loved him a long time ago. She didn't want to fall in love with him again.....

Dear Reader,

As a very special treat this season, Silhouette Desire is bringing you the best in holiday stories. It's our gift from us—the editorial staff at Silhouette—to you, the readers. The month begins with a very special MAN OF THE MONTH from Ann Major, *A Cowboy Christmas*. Years ago, a boy and girl were both born under the same Christmas star. She grew up rich; he grew up poor…and when they met, they fell into a love that would last a lifetime….

Next, Anne McAllister's CODE OF THE WEST series continues with *Cowboys Don't Stay*, the third book in her series about the Tanner brothers.

Christmas weddings are always a lot of fun, and that's why we're bringing you *Christmas Wedding* by Pamela Macaluso. And if Texas is a place you'd like to spend the holidays—along with a sexy Texas man—don't miss *Texas Pride* by Barbara McCauley. Next, popular Silhouette Romance writer Sandra Steffen makes her Desire debut with *Gift Wrapped Dad*.

Finally, do not miss *Miracles and Mistletoe,* another compelling love story from the talented pen of Cait London.

So, from our "house" to yours…Happy Holidays.

Lucia Macro

Please address questions and book requests to:
Silhouette Reader Service
U.S.: 3010 Walden Ave., P.O. Box 1325, Buffalo, NY 14269
Canadian: P.O. Box 609, Fort Erie, Ont. L2A 5X3

SANDRA STEFFEN
GIFT WRAPPED DAD

SILHOUETTE *Desire*®
Published by Silhouette Books
America's Publisher of Contemporary Romance

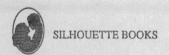 SILHOUETTE BOOKS

ISBN 0-373-05972-8

GIFT WRAPPED DAD

Copyright © 1995 by Sandra E. .Steffen

Books by Sandra Steffen

Silhouette Desire

Gift Wrapped Dad #972

Silhouette Romance

Child of Her Dreams #1005
*Bachelor Daddy #1028
*Bachelor at the Wedding #1045
*Expectant Bachelor #1056
Lullaby and Goodnight #1074

*Wedding Wager

SANDRA STEFFEN

Creating memorable characters is one of Sandra's favorite aspects of writing. She's always been a romantic and is thrilled to be able to spend her days doing what she loves—bringing her characters to life on her computer screen.

Sandra grew up in Michigan, the fourth of ten children, all of whom have taken the old adage "Go forth and multiply" quite literally. Add to this her husband, who is her real-life hero, their four school-age sons who keep their lives in constant motion, their gigantic cat, Percy, and her wonderful friends, in-laws and neighbors, and what do you get? Chaos, of course, but also a wonderful sense of belonging she wouldn't trade for the world.

Dedicated to:
My brothers, Leon, Larry, Dave and Ron—
great guys, one and all.

Acknowledgment:
A special thank-you to Gordon Allen of
Gordon Allen Rehabilitation Associates

Dear Santa,
I know it's only October, but my best friend Stephanie told me I'd have a better chance if I wrote to you before the Christmas rush. Mom's always telling me I'm a good boy. Mrs. Hansen, my teacher, said I'm not only good, I'm gifted. That means I'm smart, so you can bring me some books to read if you want to. But what I really want is a baseball glove. Not a sissy one, but a real leather, major league baseball glove. I want a dog, too. I don't care what kind. Oh, and a dad, if you know of any extras anywhere.

Yours truly,
Tommy Wilson

P.S. Stephanie says hi.

One

Will Sutherland stopped in the doorway, the hum of an exercise machine obliterating any sound he might have made. The room was oblong, with mirrors and exercise equipment lining one entire wall. It was unoccupied, except for Krista.

She was wearing a black leotard and tights, the muscles in her thighs tightening with every stride she took on the treadmill. Her hands grasped the side rails loosely. Even so, the strength in her upper arms was clearly evident.

Her hair was as dark as always, but longer, coiled into a braid partway down her back. Her face was tipped up, and her eyes were closed, which explained the fact that she hadn't noticed his presence. She was more slender than he remembered, but the way she filled out the top of her leotard was still the closest thing to perfection he'd ever seen. Will wouldn't have minded staring at her for hours, except he was in a hurry to get this matter settled.

Gathering his thoughts, he said, "I didn't believe it when they told me I'd find you up here. 'Krista, exercising?' I said. I was sure they had you confused with somebody else."

Krista Wilson opened her eyes. She didn't need to turn her head to know who had spoken; she'd recognize that voice anywhere. Breathing deeply, she slowed her pace on the treadmill and turned her head slightly, finally looking at the man who was watching her from the doorway. Studying his face unhurriedly, she couldn't help smiling.

"Hello, Will."

For a long moment he looked back at her, his lips slowly lifting into a grin she remembered well, the kind of grin that had made her swoon once, the kind of grin that reporters liked, fans loved and women adored. On anyone else, it would have looked practiced. On Will, it looked boyishly natural. It always had.

Thoughts whispered through her mind the way memories sometimes did. Images of her and Will laughing together and loving together lingered around the edges of her memory as if it had been weeks since she'd seen him instead of years. His hair was cut short, the front slightly askew, as always. His eyes were still a vivid blue—bedroom blue, according to the papers. His arms and shoulders looked as powerful as she remembered, and she could practically feel the afternoon stubble on his chin. He looked nearly the same as he had eight years ago. Only the crutches were different.

"I heard about the accident," she said quietly.

Will inclined his head, his smile changing slightly as he said, "I don't recall receiving any Get Well cards from you."

"I don't remember receiving any letters from you eight years ago, either," she said quietly.

"You never were one to beat around the bush, Krista. That's why I'm here."

He looked into her eyes as if he were reaching into her thoughts, and Krista altered her first impression of him. He wasn't the same as he'd been eight years ago. He was more serious, more mature.

Her heart was beating hard from her workout. Breathing between parted lips, she flipped a switch on the treadmill, stepped off the machine and walked closer. Fleetingly, she wished she was wearing something less revealing. Since there was nothing she could do about it, she squared her shoulders and stopped a few paces from him. With her hands on her hips, she asked, "Why are you here, Will?"

"I need a good physical therapist. And I've heard you're the best," he answered.

"You already have a physical therapist. I saw you together in *Person* Magazine. I believe her name was Miss July."

One corner of his mouth rose, but it wasn't the cocky smile she remembered. In a voice edged with irony, he said, "Unfortunately, my *former* therapist was more interested in getting me on my back than on my feet."

His eyes had darkened like smoke, and he leaned on his crutches as if he was tired to the bone. He took a deep breath and finally broke the silence between them. "You aren't going to ask, are you?"

Krista shook her head. She knew he was referring to his ability to make love. She also knew what a delicate subject that was with patients who had suffered spinal-cord injuries. The Will she remembered had been virile and too darn sexy for her own good. The man standing before her was every bit as ruggedly handsome and sexy as he'd been in her memories.

He didn't smile, but she hadn't expected him to. He didn't come right out and say *if you want proof, come closer,* either, but it was there in the set of his shoulders, in the determination in his eyes and in the way his fingers tightened around the handrests on his crutches.

She thought about moving closer and, God help her, she did. In fact, for the first time in a long time, she was tempted to touch a man intimately, to savor his touch in return. A curious sensation swooped deep inside her, and Krista couldn't suppress the admiration she felt for Will's courage and tenacity.

In that instant, she felt as if she were twenty years old all over again, meeting Will for the first time. She'd been at the bus stop not far from Michigan State University's campus that sunny October day eight years ago. He'd taken one look at her and stopped in his tracks. Thunderstruck, he'd called it. Secretly, she'd called it love. They'd been together the rest of the year, and although he'd never promised her forever, she'd somehow believed it was what they'd have.

She could still remember how they'd both reacted to an innocent brush of their shoulders. Most of all, she could still remember how her world had rocked when he'd left her behind to play pro baseball. At first she'd dreamed he'd come back. Now he had, but not the way she'd imagined. He needed a physical therapist, not a lover.

That line of thinking brought her back to the matter at hand. Raising her chin, she looked him straight in the eye and said, "You're not a small man, Will. A male physical therapist could handle your weight and help you if you stumbled or started to fall much better than I could."

"I only want you."

It required incredible effort not to look away from the determination and the longing in his eyes. Being wanted by Will Sutherland was a heady sensation. It always had been. Eight years ago he would have accented a statement like that with a wink or a raised eyebrow. Today, he stared directly into her eyes, waiting for her answer.

The changes in him were as intriguing as the things that were the same. Krista didn't want to be intrigued by him. Intrigue had a way of leading to heartache. That thought set off a warning in her mind. She'd loved him a long time ago. She didn't want to fall in love with him again, but was already feeling the pull of his attraction.

"There are thousands of physical therapists, Will. Why did you come to me?"

Will knew what she was asking. She wanted to know why he'd come to her now, after all these years. How could he put into words how he'd felt during that split second when he'd known with frightening clarity that an out-of-control truck was going to crash into his car? How could he describe the boom of impact or the sound of breaking glass and bending steel, or what it felt like to be rushed to a hospital, unable to feel his legs? How could he describe the fear and the dread and the despair of these past three months?

But Krista wanted to know. If she was going to help him, she deserved to know.

"I was having a shouting match with my former physical therapist when Dr. Richardson, one of the doctors at the rehab center in New York, stepped into the room to intervene. I asked him if he could recommend another therapist, and he told me you were one of the best."

She raised her eyebrows a little and shrugged offhandedly as she said, "Adam Richardson consulted on a case I had a few years ago. I'm a little surprised he remembered me."

Will wasn't surprised. *He'd* never forgotten her. Thoughts of her had filtered into his mind at the oddest times these past eight years, but never as often as they had these past three months. He'd done a lot of thinking while he was in the hospital in New York. About his life. About baseball. About the woman he'd left behind. He knew he'd hurt her, and he knew he had no right to ask her to help him now. Yet here he was, trying to think of some way to convince her to do just that.

"I came to you because I want to walk again, and because you're the only person I know who really believed I could reach for the stars. I'm reaching for them again."

Krista heard the earnestness and honesty in Will's voice. He'd always called his dream of playing pro baseball reaching for the stars. Baseball was the reason he left her before. It was the reason he'd leave again. She became a physical therapist because she wanted to help people, and she knew that hadn't changed. Reaching a decision wasn't difficult, but she was afraid that protecting her heart from Will's charm a second time was going to be the most difficult thing she'd ever done.

Raising her chin another notch, she said, "You'll have to clear it with the hospital first, get doctor and insurance authorization, but if they say it's possible, I'll help you."

"I've already signed on the dotted line."

His words sent an old pain quaking through her. He'd been so sure she'd do what he wanted that he'd already signed his forms? She wondered what the people in the office thought about that. It reminded her of the way she'd felt in high school when girls had whispered about her behind their hands and boys had bragged and leered.

It required an iron will to keep from stepping back, to keep from reverting to the way she used to be, to keep from giving in to old hurts. "There's one thing you should know, Will. I'm not a sure thing anymore."

Will clamped his mouth shut and squared his shoulders. She'd removed her hands from her hips and wrapped them around her waist as she'd spoken. Her voice hadn't faltered, but her stance was one of self-defense if he'd ever seen one. There had always been a sensitivity deep in the center of Krista's heart, a vulnerability and softness that was damned near impossible not to react to. She'd said *sure thing* as if they were dirty words, like *tramp* or *easy*. She'd never been any of those things. Lusty and vibrant and the hottest thing either side of the Rockies, but not easy. Memories of the way she'd responded to him, of her earthy sexuality and sumptuous body played through his mind. Hell and damnation, he was getting worked up just thinking about the way they'd been together. Looking back now, he wondered how he'd ever managed to leave her behind all those years ago.

Gazing at her this afternoon, he decided that his memories hadn't really done her justice. She'd always been great-looking, but today she was beautiful. She had dark lashes and dark eyebrows, but her eyes were the darkest of all. He watched those eyes, searching for hidden meaning. What he found in her gaze was warmth, and a hint of concern. It was that concern that brought him back to his senses.

He hadn't seen her in eight years. A lot had happened since college. She wasn't wearing a wedding ring, and her last name was still the same. But in this day and age, she could still be married. Even if she wasn't, a woman like her was bound to be involved with someone. Will Sutherland might have been a cad now and then, but no matter what, he'd always had scruples. Besides, from now on he'd be seeing her every day. He'd have time to learn about her personal life later. Right now, he had to concentrate on getting out of these cursed leg braces.

"Would you be willing to start tomorrow?" he asked.

She nodded, and Will felt his skin tighten over his knuckles as he gripped his crutches. She'd agreed to work with him. The knowledge settled inside him like hope.

After saying goodbye, he pulled himself around, making his way toward the elevator at the end of the hall, certain it wasn't his imagination that made the trek seem shorter than it had when he'd come. Adrenaline pumped through his body as he punched the elevator button. It was a lot like the surge of adrenaline he used to feel before every game. For the first time in the three months since his accident, Will thought he had a chance to make it back—on his feet, and on with his life.

Krista slipped her dripping raincoat from her shoulders and hurried into the lounge. "Coffee," she called. "I need coffee."

All three of the other people in the room stopped whispering and turned around.

"What's going on?" she asked. "Did one of you win the lottery?"

"We're not the lucky ones!" Heather Jones, a tall, willowy redhead declared. "You are. Have you seen who your ten o'clock patient is?"

Krista eyed her three co-workers who were blocking her view of the big schedule board on the wall. Reaching for the coffee, she said, "Since I just walked in and I don't have X-ray vision, I have to say no, I haven't seen who my ten o'clock patient is." But she had a pretty good idea.

"Billy the Kid," Brody Calhoun, the only man in the room, cut in.

Krista took her first sip of strong coffee, eyeing her friends over the rim of her cup. "I think you mean Will Sutherland," she said quietly.

"Call him what you want," Heather sputtered. "The fact is the most eligible bachelor within a hundred miles is going to be yours for two hours every day."

Krista sucked in a breath of air, trying to cool her tongue, which she'd burned on her coffee the instant Heather had said that Will *was going to be hers for two hours every day*. Her tongue cooled. Her thoughts didn't.

"I thought I was the most eligible bachelor for miles around," Brody grumbled.

"Oh, please," Heather said to Brody. "Your bachelorhood is so confirmed it might as well be carved in stone. What I want to know is why *Krista* gets Billy the Kid. She doesn't even *like* men for heaven's sake!"

"Now, now," Mrs. A, the only person in the room with snow-white hair, said. "Krista likes men. Don't you, Krista?"

"Yeah, right," Heather and Brody said at the same time.

"I've never been able to get to first base with her," Brody added indignantly.

"Well, that's not so unbelievable," Heather retorted, batting her eyelashes at Brody. "You're not as young as you used to be."

Krista laughed out loud at the look of horror that crossed Brody's face. Her fellow physical therapist had recently celebrated his thirty-eighth birthday. He'd discovered a gray hair a few days later and hadn't been the same since.

"What do you mean?" he insisted. "I can do anything I used to do."

"Sure you can," Heather countered.

"Maybe it's only fitting that the person who'll get to first base with Krista is a baseball player," Mrs. A said, interrupting Brody and Heather's bantering.

"Mrs. A!" Krista protested, trying to keep her coffee from sloshing over the side of her mug.

Heather and Brody both laughed, heading toward the door. Looking over her shoulder, Heather said, "I wish I had bought a lottery ticket, Krista. If I won, I'd trade it for spending two hours alone with Billy the Kid."

"Two hours!" Brody called. "That's a lot of batting practice, if you know what I mean."

"We always know what you mean, Brody," Mrs. A said, clucking her tongue. "But therapy is what we're here for, and I think it's time we all got to work." Blue eyes twinkling, the older woman cast Krista an affectionate smile and left the room.

Alone with her coffee, Krista looked at the schedule board on the wall. Mrs. A had become the volunteer coordinator for the entire wing in July. Since then, Krista had become accustomed to the other woman's rather strange speech patterns, but the way she'd implied that Will would get to first base with her had still taken her by surprise. Now that she thought about it, Mrs. A hadn't even implied it. She'd said it as if she knew. It was downright disconcerting, almost as disconcerting as Krista's erotic dreams had been all night long. In her dreams, Will had gotten a lot farther than first base, and the fans hadn't been the ones cheering.

Taking another sip of her coffee, she decided then and there to make sure that particular dream never became reality. She reminded herself that Will had come to her because he wanted to walk again, not because he wanted *her* again. She didn't know whether to be relieved or disappointed.

"Okay, Will," Krista said after she'd explained the rehabilitation center's policies and procedures. "Let's see what you can do."

"I want to try to walk without these damn leg braces, that's what I want to do."

She heard the vehemence in his voice. Underneath, she also heard the worry. She'd read his chart carefully. News of the car accident that had left Billy the Kid, the golden boy from Nebraska whose cockiness and down-home charm had melted the hearts of baseball fans everywhere, had made national headlines three months ago. Today, she'd read the doctor's version of his spinal injury. Periodically interspersed with notes about his progress were inferences to his bullheadedness and determination.

Crouching down close to the floor in front of his chair, she said, "I know you do. I want you to walk without those braces, too. That's why you're here. And that's why we're going to do this my way."

Will's blue eyes were narrowed, his chin set stubbornly. After a long silence, he said, "Three months ago the doctors thought I'd never get out of a wheelchair. Two weeks ago the therapist in New York took the liberty to tell me that she doubted I'd ever walk without crutches."

Stilling her hand on the strap of his leg brace, she said, "Then she was wrong. If you say you're going to walk again, I believe you will."

Will hadn't realized he'd been holding his breath until he noticed a burning sensation deep in his lungs. He let out that breath and took another, a sense of awe filling him. It was going to be all right. Krista wasn't going to restrict his rehabilitation. He was going to be up and walking on his own in no time.

Her hand felt warm where it rested on his thigh as she loosened the straps of his leg braces. In his mind's eye, he flexed the muscle beneath her palm.

In reality, nothing moved.

Until three months ago Will "Billy the Kid" Sutherland, had been considered the fastest base runner in pro baseball. Today he couldn't even move one tiny muscle. Squaring his shoulders and straightening his spine, he decided he'd better take things one step at a time. He'd work on walking first. And then he'd work on running.

Half an hour later he was ready to scream in frustration. He was exhausted, and he'd barely done anything. His muscles refused to work no matter what he tried. He sat in a chair, gripping the armrest while Krista issued commands.

"Push against my hand. Push. Not from the hip. Use your leg muscles. Push."

Nothing happened. He had some movement in his toes and all the feeling in his legs had come back, but without the braces his thigh and calf muscles were mush.

"Try it again. Push."

Will tried it again, with no better results. He strained every muscle that moved, from his neck all the way down to his lower abdomen. He'd pulled his ham string sliding into third base during his first season with the Cougars. Today, no matter how hard he imagined it, no matter how hard he *worked,* he couldn't make any of the muscles in his legs push against Krista's hands. He wanted to learn to walk, dammit, but after forty-five minutes, all he felt was more frustrated than ever.

"Come on," she said. "That's it. Concentrate. Push. Again. Push."

"I am pushing," he ground out between clenched teeth.

Krista glanced up into Will's face. His brow was glistening with sweat. Beads of perspiration dotted his upper lip. His teeth were clenched as if he wanted to bite somebody's head off. She had a feeling that somebody was her. Good. She could deal with anger. In fact, it was a great motivator.

"If you want to get mad, go ahead," she said. "This is going to take time, and your anger is going to help you get through it. You've made remarkable progress, and I'm sure you'll continue to— "

"Don't patronize me, all right? I got enough of that from Miss July!"

After a moment of silence, a sheepish expression stole across his face. She watched his shoulders move and his chest expand as he drew in a deep breath and said, "I guess I'm a little edgy."

This was the Will she remembered. A little arrogant, a little cocky, and underneath it all, maddeningly sweet.

"Don't worry about it," she replied levelly. "One whole semester in college was dedicated to dealing with ornery, pigheaded patients."

His blue eyes reflected the overhead lighting as he said, "Who are you calling ornery?"

Krista noticed he didn't dispute the pigheaded portion of her statement and couldn't help smiling. In that moment, the years seemed to fall away. She felt just as exasperated and infatuated with Will as she'd been when they were both young.

On impulse, she ran her finger along the bottom of his long foot. His heel jerked out of her hand, landing on the floor with a soft thud. She looked from his toes to his face and found his eyes mirroring her own surprise.

"You moved your leg!" she said from her position on the floor.

Featherlike laugh lines crinkled around his eyes, and a wondrous smile pulled at his mouth. Her instinctive reaction to him was powerful, nearly as powerful as the silent communication that passed between them. The shock of it ran through her body. Their gazes locked, and their breathing came in unison.

He reached for both her hands, slowly drawing her up toward him. Steadying herself against his chest, she spread her fingers wide across the expanse of strong muscles. His hand grazed her face, his fingers sliding into the hair near her ear. His eyes were half closed, his expression dreamily intimate. She breathed between parted lips, her eyelashes fluttering down the instant his lips touched hers.

The touch of his mouth on hers brought back so many feelings that tears moistened her eyelashes and a knot rose to her throat. He pulled her closer, his thighs straddling her, his arms wrapped snugly around her back, making her body respond in an achingly familiar way. For a moment, time stood still, and there was nothing in the world but this instant with this man.

Gradually, some thread of rationality filtered through her fragmented thoughts. Will was sitting in a hospital chair in a hospital room. Good heavens, he was her patient.

Krista jumped to her feet and spun around, pacing to the far side of the room. "That can't happen again," she cried, amazed to hear the huskiness in her own voice.

"I think it could."

His deep, husky voice took her back to the old days, when kisses like the one they'd just shared had happened every day. Her memories calmed her in ways she hadn't expected. This wasn't the end of the world. Sure, she'd kissed a patient, but it hadn't been just any patient. This was a man she'd once loved, a man who could still ignite her desire in three seconds or less.

Taking a deep breath, she tried again. "Let me rephrase my statement. That *won't* happen again."

"That isn't going to be nearly as much fun."

His simple reply brought her head up. The kiss they'd shared had been a natural, spontaneous reaction, just as the movement of Will's foot had been a natural reaction to being tickled.

"You may be right," she said, hating the way her voice caught on the last word. "But you're my patient. And I don't kiss patients."

"Do you mean I'm the first patient you've ever kissed?"

"The first. And the last. I'm not like your Miss July. I'm not a package deal. I'll be your physical therapist, but this time, our relationship will remain strictly professional."

He seemed to digest her words, his gaze trailing down her body as he said, "That isn't going to be easy. When you touch me, I find myself wanting to touch you back."

His honesty was wreaking havoc with her senses. She hoped he didn't notice the quaver in her voice as she said, "I have to touch you. I have to help you get those muscles to move. You can touch me back, Will. As long as you remain friendly and professional."

He was looking at his left leg, which allowed her a moment to study him unobserved. He was wearing baggy gray sweatpants and a New York Titans T-shirt. She knew his legs were weak from his spinal injury, but they didn't look it. His upper body was powerfully muscular, his chest and shoulders broad. A vein ran up his forearm, only to disappear inside the sleeve of his shirt.

The bruising to his spinal column had been traumatic, but Will hadn't sat around sulking. A person didn't acquire this kind of muscle tone that way. Yesterday he'd told her he'd come to her because she was the only person who could make him reach for the stars. Now Krista realized that wasn't true. With or without her, he'd always reached for the stars.

The Will she'd known back in college had been on the wild side, but even then he'd been completely motivated.

He'd run track to increase his speed and stamina and practiced his swing, his throw and his slide. He'd never been the kind of man who enjoyed inactivity. This type of injury was terrifying to everyone, but to a man like Will, it must have been ten times worse. Krista eyed his crutches and leg braces lying next to his chair, her admiration growing. He hadn't taken it sitting down, at least not for long.

Trying for a friendly yet professional tone of voice, she said, "We used to touch each other a lot, and old habits die hard. But I'm your physical therapist now, and you're my patient. I think we need to establish some ground rules, things that are safe, and things that are off limits. Kissing me is off limits."

He started to speak, but she interrupted. "Don't look so stricken. I've sworn off all men, not just you."

With that, she strode to the wall and grasped the handles on a lightweight wheelchair. "Come on," she said, pushing the chair toward him. "Let's take a ride down to the patient exercise room. You still have an hour of time left this morning. Let's put it to good use."

Will eyed the gray chair dazedly. He was aware that it was there, but his mind couldn't seem to get past the fact that Krista had just told him she'd sworn off men. All men.

He'd known his share of women, but he'd never met anyone who was more sensuous than Krista. Back in college, she'd been as ravenous as he was. Sometimes, she'd been embarrassed about her earthy murmurs and sighs, her automatic reactions and responses to their lovemaking. He used to love to kiss her embarrassment away, to make her forget the inhibitions instilled in her by that prissy family of hers, to take her to the brink of completion, then watch her soar. He never would have imagined that a healthy, vibrant, sexy woman like Krista would swear off men. Not in a million years. But then, he never would have imagined nearly dying in a car accident three months ago, either, or perhaps never being able to walk again.

Eyeing the wheelchair, he said, "I spent the worst two months of my life trying to get out of one of those contraptions and now you want me to get back in?"

She shrugged in an offhand way and said, "I thought you were here to learn to walk again, but if you want to take the time to get into your leg braces so that you don't have to ride in a wheelchair, suit yourself."

He stared at her for a silence-filled moment, then grasped the chair's armrest. "I hate it when you're right."

"I know," she said as she leaned down to set the brake.

Her breast brushed against his forearm, the hair on his arm standing up at the brief contact. Slowly, his eyes moved upward, coming to rest on her face. Since Krista wasn't very tall, it wasn't a far climb, but it sure was a pleasant one. Will sucked in a quick breath as the intensity of her gaze hit him between the eyes. He'd reacted to her this way before, lots of times. He hadn't seen or talked to her in eight years, but he hadn't forgotten her. He was honest enough to know that he'd experienced some of the best sex of his life when Krista had been in his arms. Fleetingly, he wondered how he'd ever managed to leave her all those years ago.

Thoughts crystallized in his mind as he recalled a comment she'd made when he'd first seen her yesterday. *I don't remember receiving any letters from you eight years ago.*

She'd only been twenty-one years old back then, but she'd loved him the way a woman loves a man. He'd loved her, too, he supposed. But he'd been a young twenty-two, his sights set on the major leagues, not on the woman with an unfailing spirit and unfathomable brown eyes.

Will grasped the other armrest and levered himself into the wheelchair. She bent to release the brake, her clean scent filling his nostrils. Before she straightened, he asked, "Did you swear off men because of me, Krista?"

The chair's brake let go just as her breath pierced the silence in the room. For a moment she remained at eye level.

Her eyebrows were arched and her voice was clipped as she said, "Don't flatter yourself, Will."

She straightened, pulling the chair back with more force than might have been necessary. Will let out a loud whoop as she pushed him through the wide doorway. *"Don't flatter yourself,"* she'd said. Krista never had been one for trite lines or inane white lies. Her honesty was refreshing, but then she'd always been refreshing.

He used to tell her so. Will smiled to himself as he remembered what she'd told him in return. "I'm refreshing, and you're fresh. Quite a combination, don't you think?"

Krista called hello to other patients as they passed. Will barely noticed. His thoughts were elsewhere, deep in the *fresh* zone, where images danced through him mind, images of him and Krista in his dorm room, and later, in her tiny apartment just off campus.

"Mommy! Mommy!"

He turned his head slowly as a young boy with dark hair and huge brown eyes ran toward him from the opposite end of the hall. Will glanced around, searching for the object of the child's gaze.

"Mommy, guess what?"

It took Will a moment to realize that the kid was talking to Krista. *Mommy?* Krista was somebody's mother?

"Tommy," Krista called. "Where's Mrs. Hall?"

"She's coming," the child replied. "See? Back there."

Will didn't know why he glanced down the hall, but sure enough, a heavyset woman with frizzy brown hair was hurrying toward them.

"You're Billy the Kid!" the boy exclaimed, staring at Will.

"Tommy," Krista admonished, "where are your manners? This is Mr. Sutherland. Mr. Sutherland, my son, Tommy."

Will heard the pride and affection in Krista's voice as she spoke to her son. The little urchin extended his right hand,

and in his befuddled state, Will enfolded the boy's fingers in his own large hand. "Hi, Tommy. How ya doing?"

"Cool," the child said in awe. "Wait until I tell Stephanie that I shook hands with Billy the Kid. She's my friend. She doesn't care much about baseball, so she doesn't know you stole forty-two bases last season, but she's still pretty smart."

By the time the boy had finished talking, Mrs. Hall had joined him and Krista in the middle of the corridor. Krista spoke to the older woman, and Tommy rattled on about home runs and batting averages. Within minutes, Mrs. Hall was leading Tommy away. This time the child's hand was tucked firmly in hers.

Will sat statue still, barely conscious of the lady with the walker who was steadily drawing closer. "How old is your son?" he asked.

"Tommy's six going on thirty," Krista replied. "He's gifted."

Will digested that statement easily enough. Since she had a six-year-old son, obviously she hadn't sworn off men immediately after he'd left eight years ago. Yesterday, he'd assumed that Krista wasn't married. The subject hadn't crossed his mind today, especially not while he'd been kissing her. She said she'd sworn off men. Exactly what had she meant by that?

"Uh, Krista?" he asked, waving at the little boy at the end of the hall.

"Mm?" she asked, waving, too.

"Are you married?"

Two

Are you married?

The question hung in her mind as the faint swish, thud, swish, thud of a walker steadily drew near. She'd assumed Will knew her marital status. After all, he'd shown up at the Fourth Street Rehab Center in Allentown so sure she'd agree to be his physical therapist that he'd signed his outpatient admittance forms before talking to her.

She'd been fighting her reaction to seeing him again since the first moment she'd looked into his eyes yesterday. It was so easy to get emotionally involved with her patients, to share in their grief and in their achievements. The fact that she'd known Will intimately eight years ago made her even more susceptible to emotional involvement. Somehow she had to find a way to help him regain the use of his legs and retain her own equilibrium at the same time. That wasn't going to be easy.

Oh, no, she thought to herself. That wasn't going to be easy at all. She hadn't been on an even keel since yesterday, but she hadn't realized just how much Will had affected her until she'd seen Tommy running toward her a few minutes ago. She'd known he had the day off from school, and she'd known he and Mrs. Hall were going to stop by later this morning. But while she'd been working with Will, Krista had lost all track of time and had forgotten about Tommy's visit. That hadn't happened before, but then she hadn't been kissed senseless by one of her patients before, either. From now on, she was going to have to stay on her toes and try to keep one step ahead of Will.

She watched as Tommy and Mrs. Hall disappeared through the door at the end of the corridor. Grasping the handles on Will's chair, Krista finally answered his question. "I'm not married."

Will turned around in his chair to look up at her. "That must make those tight-a—"

His eyes darted to the left, and he let the soft *a* sound trail away into thin air. Understanding dawned as she followed his gaze and noticed that Mrs. Felpont, Heather's elderly patient, had moved within hearing distance.

"Er, make that those tight-lipped sisters of yours feel like gloating even more."

Krista smiled at Mrs. Felpont, wondering how many men these days would have cleaned up their language because a kindly gray-haired lady was nearby. Once again she fought her rising sense of wonder.

Staring down into Will's eyes, she couldn't help noticing the derision in his expression. He never had thought much of her sisters. She shook her head in answer to his question, deciding not to go on to explain that she didn't have a lot of contact with her family anymore. Not that she'd ever had much in common with them in the first place.

"Come on, Krista," he said, drawing her back to the present. "We have less than an hour left for my therapy today. If we want to get me on my feet, we have to get moving."

Krista hurried after Will, thinking it wasn't going to be easy to stay one step ahead of this man. The fact that he couldn't walk made absolutely no difference whatsoever.

She caught up with him inside the double doors and found him looking all around. In one corner of the room, another therapist was helping a young girl into a whirlpool tub. Brody was barking encouragement to a large black man who was lifting weights. Heather was working with Mrs. Felpont, and still another with a teenage boy.

Krista glanced down at Will's face. His grin had slipped away and had been replaced with a serious expression people rarely associated with Billy the Kid. He really was different in many ways. She wondered if the years had changed him, or if the accident had.

"Come on," she said. "Let's get you loosened up."

He glanced from one end of her body to the other. By the time it came back to her face, the seriousness had left his expression. "I thought you'd never ask."

She felt a tingling in the pit of her stomach and a grudging smile on her lips. Will always had been able to turn an innocent phrase into something provocative. She was definitely going to have a hard time keeping one step ahead of him. The surprising thing was, she was looking forward to it.

He set the brake on his wheelchair and placed one hand on the chair's armrest and the other hand on the low table, swinging himself over with amazing ease. Krista moved the wheelchair out of the way and said, "Lie on your back with your head on that pillow. I'm going to stretch your muscles and help keep those joints limber."

Will did as she instructed, lying back and grasping the handrails to maneuver himself up to the top of the table. Krista started with his right leg, lifting it, rotating it, bending his knee and pushing toward his body. Her touch was firm yet gentle, and he tried to imagine that his muscles were moving on their own.

"I know this is uncomfortable," she said. "Tell me if it becomes unbearable."

He watched her intently as he said, "Three months ago I couldn't feel anything from my waist down. Believe me, a little discomfort isn't a bad thing."

She continued to work on him, pulling gently, then twisting and pushing. At one point, she tucked his ankle under her arm, the side of her breast cushioning his lower leg like a feather pillow. Using her body for leverage, she leaned forward, bending his knee, then straightening his leg.

"How does that feel?" she asked, repeating the exercise.

His gaze skimmed her breasts before settling on her face. "That feels great."

She nodded and continued with his therapy.

"Let's talk," he said, his voice catching on the last word as she pressed his bent knee toward his body.

"All right. Let's start by establishing those ground rules I mentioned earlier."

"Ground rules, huh? I suppose I can assume that asking about your sex life is off limits?"

Her eyes narrowed speculatively. "I've already told you I've sworn off men. Even if I hadn't, that particular topic would definitely be off limits."

"Okay, why don't you tell me what you're wearing underneath that cute little uniform?"

He winced as she twisted his leg, and even though her attention appeared to be completely trained on his knee, Will caught her little smile. After a long pause, he finally said, "Then tell me about your son."

That brought a bigger smile to her lips. "Tommy's a great kid," she said, moving to the other side of the table, where she began to repeat the entire procedure with his left leg. "Like I said, he's six going on thirty. We live in Coopersburg, a small town about twelve miles from here."

"You said he's gifted. That must make your family happy."

Her touch remained gentle while she worked his left leg, but her voice contained a strange edge of irony as she said, "Actually, they don't approve of the way I'm raising him."

"What's not to approve of? He looks pretty happy to me. He knows baseball and he looks just like you."

"That was the first thing I did wrong," she answered. "I gave him my genes."

"Those are some genes, if you don't mind my saying so."

Instead of smiling the way he'd expected, she remained completely serious. "I'm sure they would have preferred it if he'd been tall and blond and straitlaced like they are."

He scowled to himself. Krista's family probably didn't approve of the fact that Tommy liked baseball, either. Her sisters sounded just as huffy and highfalutin as they always had. It didn't sound as if Katrina, Kimberly or Kendra had changed over the past eight years.

"Tommy looks like a well-adjusted, impish little kid. I'd say you should be proud."

Krista heard the depth of sincerity in Will's voice. Looking from his legs straight into his eyes, she lowered herself to the table next to him, lowering her eyes at the same time. "Do you know what makes me the most proud?"

"What?" he asked softly.

"The fact that he's having a normal childhood." She glanced at him to see if he understood and found him watching her closely. "I mean, I know he's exceptionally bright. After all, he's only six years old and he's already in the second grade. But he likes baseball and soccer as well as playing the violin. He has a new little friend. Her name is Stephanie, and even though most boys his age have other boys for their best friend—"

"You said he was smart," Will cut in.

Krista rolled her eyes and began kneading the muscles in his calf, slowly working her way up his leg. "I never know what to expect from that boy. Even though his reasoning skills are amazing, he still believes in Santa Claus."

"Doesn't everybody?"

Krista felt a smile steal through her, thinking it was ironic that she'd told Will that Tommy was six going on thirty, when Will was thirty going on six.

She heard Will clear his throat and call her name. For a moment she wondered why his voice had gone so low, so husky, so deep.

"Uh, Krista?" he said, finally breaking into her reverie. "You're getting awfully close to a particularly sensitive part of my anatomy."

She came back from her musings with a start. He was right. Her hands had wandered awfully close to... a place that was definitely off limits. "Sorry about that," she whispered.

"Believe me, I don't mind," he answered. "It's just that if you keep it up, I'm going to pull you on top of me and finish what you started."

"Is that what you did with Miss July?" she asked, mentally kicking herself for letting her curiosity show.

He took his time tucking his hands underneath his head. His eyes had darkened, taking on an intense expression, as he said, "Now *you've* stumbled onto a topic that's off limits."

She turned from her task and laughed unexpectedly, a spontaneous, deep, pleasant laugh that was the essence of the woman herself, a laugh that made a man think of other activities even more spontaneous, even more pleasant. Will was aware that other people in the room had turned when they'd heard Krista's laughter. More than anything, he was aware of the way the throaty sound had sneaked inside his body, and the way the touch of her hands had sneaked up his thigh. Both felt good.

Lowering his leg to the table, she said, "I know you still have some time left for therapy today, but I think we've just about covered everything for the first session. Come on. I'll push you back to the room where we started. Tomorrow, we'll pick up where we left off.''

Without saying a word, he sat up and maneuvered himself back into the wheelchair. She'd said that tomorrow they'd pick up where they left off. Will was pretty sure she hadn't meant where they'd left off eight years ago.

For the millionth time these past three months he wondered what his life would have been like if he hadn't gotten behind the wheel of that rental car last July. What if he'd seen the out-of-control truck sooner? What if he never regained all his movement? What if this was as good as he'd ever be?

No. Will wouldn't concentrate on what if. He'd survived the car accident. He'd gotten his feeling back, and bit by bit he'd regain his strength. He knew he should count his blessings in another area, too. His sex drive was intact. In fact, he couldn't remember the last time he'd been so aware of his raging hormones. Maybe it was because of Krista.

There was one *what if* he didn't mind thinking about. Krista undoubtedly had good reasons for swearing off all men. What if he was the one man who could change her mind?

Every few seconds, Will punched another channel on the TV's remote control. Situation comedies didn't appeal to him tonight. Neither did rescue or cop shows. An action movie caught his attention briefly, but after only minutes he flipped to the next station. In a moment of undiluted annoyance, he punched the Off button and jumped to his feet. At least that's what his brain told his body to do. Swearing under his breath, he reached for his crutches and pulled himself up to a standing position.

A primitive panic wrapped its fingers around his throat and threatened to cut off his breathing. Damn. He hated this god-awful inability to move on his own. Tiny rooms didn't faze him, and small spaces had always made him feel cozy.

But this was different. This paralysis closed in on him like moving walls in horror movies.

Will grasped his crutches and maneuvered around the room, cursing the panic out loud until his breathing returned to normal and his thoughts calmed. He stopped at the sliding door in his first-floor apartment. Peering through the rain-speckled glass, he noticed lights coming on across the street. Standing there all alone in his apartment, which contained some of the most modern conveniences money could buy, he wondered if he should have taken his mother up on her offer to come and stay with him until he was back on his feet.

In his mind, he pictured the Nebraska sun glinting off the whitewashed buildings back home. It was harvest time, and his father and brother would probably be walking toward the house right about now, the day's dust thick on their skin. Inside, his mother would have a huge meal prepared. Voices would rise and fall during supper as Cort and their father argued about the price of wheat and just about everything else under the sun. In comparison, Will's furnished apartment here in Allentown seemed as quiet as a crypt, and just as confining.

His family had wanted him to come home for the rest of his rehabilitation. Will knew they'd have done everything in their power to help him. That's why he hadn't gone. If he had let them do everything for him, he knew he'd never make it all the way back. That's why he'd decided to come to Krista. She'd force him to reach his full potential. She always had.

Krista.

He glanced behind him at the gray carpet and the gray walls and the gray curtains and the gray sofa. Even the air looked gray. He remembered the way Krista's pink lips had lifted when she smiled, the way her brown eyes had glinted when she laughed and the way her cheeks had colored when he'd asked about her sex life. Nothing about Krista was gray. Not her appearance, certainly not her personality.

Will thought about the past two days, remembering everything about her, the way she moved, what she said, even the way she said it. The intricate details in his memories surprised him. He was usually hard-pressed to put a name with a face. Yet in eight years, he hadn't forgotten anything about her.

Not that she was exactly the same as he remembered. There was a subtle difference in her smiles, and he was sure he'd never heard so much pride and love in her voice as he'd heard today when she'd talked about her son. She said they lived in Coopersburg, a small town twelve miles away. For the heck of it, Will took out the telephone directory and turned to the area maps.

He located Coopersburg on Highway 309, and wondered what sort of town it was. He wondered what her house looked like. Out of the blue, he wondered what was stopping him from finding out.

Twenty minutes later he eased the midsize car around the last corner, steering with his left hand, accelerating and braking with his right. This specially made car served its purpose, but he couldn't wait to drive his midnight blue sports car with four on the floor and raised-letter tires.

He slowed down when he spotted the house with the number he was looking for. *So this is where Krista lives.* The house sat on the corner, the streetlight reflecting off forest green siding and a black roof and shutters. A red bicycle leaned against the garage and wet leaves covered the compact yard. A small scarecrow hung from a Happy Halloween sign on the front door, and a ceramic black cat sat on the bottom step.

For a moment, he simply stared at the small house. He hadn't called first, and he hadn't been invited. That had never stopped him before. With anticipation strumming through him, he pulled the keys from the ignition, reached for his crutches and opened the door.

Leaves squished beneath his feet as he made his way to the front door, the panic that had threatened to choke him half an hour ago nearly gone. Now another sensation mingled with the restlessness in his mind and chest, this one infinitely more enjoyable.

He knocked on the door, deciding to say something clever and nonchalant the moment Krista opened it. He saw a curtain flutter and heard the lock turn. His anticipation increased and he felt himself begin to smile.

The door opened, but his words caught in his chest. All Will could do was stare.

Krista's hair was down, waving past her shoulders like a dark cloud. The porch light deepened the color of her eyes and made the skin on her face look almost translucent.

"Will, are you all right?"

He nodded woodenly.

"Then, what are you doing here?" she asked.

"I had to get out of that apartment before it swallowed me alive." Was that his voice, so hazy and far away?

"That's understandable," she said. "You always were a man of action. Come on in."

The soft rustle of her long purple shirt brought him out of his befuddled state. Taking a deep breath, he mentally kicked himself. So much for sweeping her away with his nonchalance. He had an almost overwhelming urge to drop his crutches and take her into his arms, to grasp her shoulders and pull her up to him for a long, drugging kiss. He wondered if she'd consider that off limits, too.

Finally he cast her what he hoped was a beguiling grin. "I thought about taking a walk, but decided to go visiting instead."

"How many people do you know in Pennsylvania?" she asked.

"Counting myself, two."

Shaking her head, Krista began to laugh. When she'd first seen Will standing on her front step, he'd looked bewildered, shaken. Why wouldn't he be? Even the most self-confident, rugged men would be rocked by the kind of injury Will had sustained.

"Nice place."

She watched as he took in the interior of her home, following his gaze as it strayed over textured wallpaper in shades of burgundy, gold and green, lighting on her overstuffed sofa and chairs and lacy curtains. He didn't stop until he'd taken in the computer in the corner, Tommy's radio-controlled car next to the couch and the baby toys she'd gotten out for her best friend's triplets to play with in the morning.

"Did you decorate this yourself?" he asked, his voice low.

She made a sound that meant yes, then said, "Decorating magazines would call this room French country."

"I'm not surprised," he said softly. "You always had a passion for anything French."

Krista looked directly into his eyes, noticing that the panic she'd seen when she'd first opened the door was gone. This was more like the Will she remembered. Catching her lower lip between her teeth, she was glad that she'd been able to help him chase the dragons away.

"French restaurants *are* my favorite," she said softly.

The stubble on his chin looked almost black in the faint light as he took a step closer. "And French bread," he added with a half smile.

She crossed her arms and held his gaze as she said, "And don't forget French toast."

His crutch clunked against the coffee table as he took another step closer. "And then there's always French kissing," he said huskily.

This time, Krista didn't add anything.

"Do you remember how much you used to love that, Krista?"

Her eyes drifted down to his mouth, and warmth drifted through her body. He had sensuous lips, masculinely shaped and boyishly pouty. Her skin heated in spite of the thin material of her shirt and jeans. That didn't keep her eyes from trailing down his neck, over his wide shoulders and powerful arms, over his chest and trim stomach. Rather than detract from his powerful physique, the crutches somehow added to his mystery. Krista doubted that anything could alter his allure.

"I remember a lot of French things," she said. "Tommy's favorite is french fries."

"He's still young."

Before she knew it, laughter bubbled out of her. "Oh, Will. Would you like to sit down?"

"I'd rather kiss you."

His honesty was like a wick, his gaze a lighted match. Together they stoked a fire within her, a fire she'd thought had been extinguished a long time ago. That fire had burned out of control once. Krista didn't plan to lose control again.

He moved toward her. This time she took a step back.

"Tommy's sleeping right down the hall."

"I wasn't planning to make a lot of noise."

His statement brought her eyebrows up. He used to make plenty of noise, and they both knew it. Holding out her hand to halt his forward movement, she said, "Will, a lot has changed since the old days. I have a different life now. I have a son and a home and work I enjoy. We both know the attraction is still between us, but if all you wanted was sex, I think you would have stayed with Miss July, don't you?"

He was leaning on his crutches, his eyes narrowing a little more with every word she said. He looked at her so long and so hard that she wondered if he could see inside her mind. Taking a deep breath, he shrugged and tilted his head to one side. After a long moment, he finally said, "Her name wasn't really Miss July."

"Oh, really? What was her name?"

"I forget."

This time her laugh was more like a snort, but it relieved the pressure inside her and lightened the moment. His little jest told her that he understood what she was trying to tell him. He understood that she couldn't let herself get involved with him, not now, not after she'd come so far. He understood, and she was grateful.

"Since I'm the only person you know in Pennsylvania, could I offer you a cup of hot chocolate?"

Will clenched his teeth, feeling a muscle move in his jaw. Her statement about the reason he'd come to Pennsylvania hit home. She was right. He hadn't come to her because he wanted to start up where they'd left off when they were young. He'd gone to the Fourth Street Rehab Center because he wanted her to help him get his strength and stamina back. He knew she wouldn't have had to agree to be his physical therapist. Yet she had. It was his turn to be grateful.

"Hot chocolate sounds great, as long as you promise to talk to me while we drink it. Those walls in my apartment really were closing in on me."

She turned so quickly that her oversize shirt fluttered behind her before settling around her thighs once again. "Hot chocolate and friendly conversation coming right up."

He assumed the fact that she continued talking meant that she expected him to follow her. He trailed after her, propping himself against the counter in her U-shaped kitchen.

"That claustrophobic sensation you're experiencing is perfectly normal. People who are paralyzed or suddenly lose their sight or hearing often experience that kind of panic," she said as she added water to the teakettle and turned on the burner.

"Does it go away?" he asked.

"Usually," she said, reaching onto a shelf for two mugs.

Will flattened his palm against the ceramic-tile counter, smoothing his hand over the cool, shiny surface. Fluffy green area rugs were scattered here and there over the vinyl floor. The table was wood, the chairs cane backed. Woven shades covered the windows, and in the middle of it all, Krista stood at the stove pouring instant hot chocolate into mugs, her hair a riot of waves, her purple shirt clinging to her softly rounded form.

"How long have you lived here?" he asked.

"Three years," she said, turning around to lean on the counter on the other side of the kitchen.

"Did you live here with Tommy's father?"

She shook her head slowly. "That relationship ended before Tommy was born. After that, my wandering days were over."

Will didn't understand why her words struck such a chord inside him. Her statement was simple enough, but it seemed to be filled with hidden meaning.

"Decorators might think this room is a little too much," she confessed, obviously attempting to change the subject. "But I like it. Most people decorate with color. I'm a texture person. It has to feel good in order for me to like it."

He saw her suck in a quick breath as if she'd just realized what she'd said. He could have said something provocative. The Lord only knew how many possibilities flitted through his mind. She'd said she was a texture person. He imagined the texture of her palm gliding over his arm, up to his shoulders and across his chest. He imagined her fingers dipping to the center of his abdomen, and *wandering* farther.

They both jumped when the teakettle whistled, then grinned sheepishly when she removed it from the burner. While she stirred boiling water into the hot cocoa mix, Will looked on, trying to get his screaming hormones in check. He wanted Krista, but he knew she was right. He hadn't come here, to Allentown in general or here tonight in particular, to start something. Besides, she'd told him in a couple of different ways that she wasn't looking for a relationship. Once she'd said she'd sworn off men. Another time she'd told him that theirs would be strictly a patient/therapist relationship. Just now, she'd offered friendship in a roundabout way. Under the circumstances, Will didn't see how he could turn it down or expect anything more.

She placed the mug of hot cocoa on the counter. Motioning to the low-backed bar stool behind him, she said, "Let's sit in here."

Will rounded the counter and leaned into the chair. After propping his crutches against the counter, he took a sip of cocoa and said, "Mmm. Tastes good."

She nodded. "Hot chocolate is okay, but I dream about coffee."

"You dream about coffee?"

She nodded again. "My one and only weakness."

Will eyed her over the rim of his mug and said, "I know, I know. You used to have two, but you gave up men."

He wasn't sure he liked the fact that men had been easier for her to give up than coffee. "I can understand why you're happy with your life, Krista. I mean, you have a cute kid and a nice house and a good job. But why would you give up men completely?"

Krista couldn't help laughing at Will's dark expression. Placing her hand on his arm, she said, "You make it sound like I gave up candy for Lent. I didn't do it for penance, Will. I did it to find my own happiness." Lifting her hand from his arm, she placed her palm over her heart.

"And did you find your own happiness?" he asked quietly.

She looked around her at her kitchen with all its textures, at the clutter on the counter near the phone, at the field-trip form she'd signed for Tommy and the refrigerator covered with his drawings. She eyed the watch she wore for work and her name badge she always put on just before she walked out the door.

"Not the kind I thought I always wanted, but yes," she replied, keenly aware of his scrutiny. "I have."

After a long silence while they both sipped their hot chocolate, she asked, "Have you?"

Will thought about her question. Had he found happiness? At times he was happy enough. He knew he was going to be thrilled when he could walk on his own again. But that wasn't what she'd meant. He'd had a happy childhood and plenty of happy times. Until these past three months, he hadn't given happiness much thought. Until tonight, he'd never put his feelings on the subject into words.

Smoothing his finger up and down the handle on his mug of hot cocoa, he said, "I was young and cocky when the Detroit Cougars drafted me into the minor leagues. When I made it to the major leagues the following year, I thought I was on top of the world, thought I was invincible. For three years, I was. Then I had a bad season, tore up my knee. My swing was off. So was my timing. Before I knew it, they traded me to the New York Titans, traded me like stamps or marbles. That brought me down a peg or two, believe me."

"That's the way of the game. You play by the rules. Nothing personal, right?" she said quietly.

Nothing personal. Will glanced sideways at her, wondering what she was thinking. "I guess pro sports is a long way from physical therapy, huh?"

"Oh, I don't know," she answered. "They both have their rules. I think people should do what they enjoy."

She tipped her mug up and drank the last of her cocoa. Mesmerized, Will stared at her slender neck as she swallowed, and then at her mouth as she flicked her tongue across her upper lip. She'd said people should do what they enjoyed. He'd *enjoy* tasting the chocolate on her lips.

His heart began to hammer in his chest and his breathing deepened as he said, "It would probably be against one of those rules to kiss you."

She nodded. A second later, she started to laugh. She'd laughed this way earlier today, spontaneous and throaty. Then, like now, the sound sneaked into his senses, reminding him of how her laughter used to trail away when he touched her. His body heated from the memories alone. How he'd love to touch her again, to slide his hands into the V-neckline of her shirt and glide it down her body. He'd love to cover her breasts with his palms, then bend to take each peak into his mouth. And then he'd swing her into his arms and stride with her to the bed....

He came back to his senses in the nick of time. He couldn't take her in his arms and carry her off to bed. He couldn't even walk without crutches. Besides, if kissing his therapist was against the rules, he had no doubt that making love with her was, too.

He finished his own hot chocolate, aware that she was watching him intently. He replaced his mug on the counter and reached for his crutches. She looked a little surprised, as if she'd expected him to kiss her anyway, or at least to try. He'd have loved to do just that. But he wouldn't, at least not yet.

She followed him as he made his way to the front door. Moving ahead of him, she opened it. Will turned on the top step, loving the surge of adrenaline pumping through his body.

"Will," she said. "I don't think I like what you're thinking."

"How do you know what I'm thinking?" he asked, the picture of innocence.

"Because I've seen that look in your eyes before," she replied. "If I remember correctly you always looked like that when you had something dirty on your mind."

He gave her a thorough once-over, silently giving her credit for being absolutely right. Rather than admitting it out loud, he said, "If you know what I'm thinking, I'm not the only one with a dirty mind."

He saw the surprise in her eyes, and the sensuality, too. What a combination.

He glanced into her living room behind her, at all the textures she loved. She had changed in many ways, but in that way she was still the same. She'd always loved to touch.

Memories of Krista's touch scattered his thoughts much like the late-night breeze was fluttering across the wet leaves on the sidewalk behind him. Like moisture soaking into those leaves, one thought soaked into his mind. In that instant, he began to wonder if maybe there had been more than one reason for his arrival in Pennsylvania.

Will had never believed in fate. He preferred to think that a person carved out his own future. But maybe fate had played a role in this, after all. Maybe fate had sent him to Krista's house tonight. One thing he knew for sure: he'd gone there with panic tied around his windpipe. Now the panic was gone and desire was pumping through his body.

He wanted Krista Wilson. He wondered if it was against the rules to shout it at the top of his lungs. Whether it was or not, he wouldn't do that. Sure, he wanted her, but if he was ever going to have her, he knew he'd have to be a lot more subtle than that.

Will suddenly felt as if this was the first inning of a brand-new game. The stands were full and the sun was shining. Billy the Kid was up to bat, and the sky was the limit. Will Sutherland was back in the game. In more ways than one.

"Good night, Krista," he said before turning around, purposefully using his deepest tone of voice.

"Will?" she asked, drawing his gaze back to hers. "I just want you to know that you're welcome to call or stop by whenever the walls start to close in on you."

He felt as if his blood were thickening to molasses, swelling his chest and heating his body. "Thanks," he said softly. "There's something I'd like you to know, too."

"What's that?"

"Miss July and I never—" He clamped his mouth shut without finishing. Where in the world had that declaration come from?

"Oh, Will," she murmured. "I'm sorry."

Will felt the adrenaline leak out of him like air from an open valve. Krista had tipped her head to one side and was looking at him as if she was genuinely sympathetic. He wanted to tell her that he wasn't sorry, that he could have made love with the other woman if he'd have wanted to. He just hadn't wanted to.

Turning away from the sympathy in her expression, he clenched his jaw and began to make his way to his car. Moments ago he'd felt as if he was standing at bat in the first inning of a brand-new game. Now it seemed as if, in the blink of an eye, the game had been rained out.

He didn't want anyone's pity, least of all Krista's. Okay, he thought to himself as he stuffed his crutches into the car and drove away. Maybe she hadn't looked at him with pity in her eyes, but there had been sympathy. And that was almost as bad.

Will tried to imagine that he was lacing up his cleats and stepping up to home plate. In his imagination, he gripped the bat in his hands, measuring its weight. Unbidden came the image of Krista's satin-covered skin filling his palms.

Scowling, he flipped on the radio and turned up the volume. He let his mind go blank as he drove back to his plain gray apartment.

Three

"Look out. Here they come!" Tommy called from the back door.

Krista tweaked Tommy's nose as her best friend, Gina Harris, somehow managed to get all three of her daughters through the door and into the kitchen. Since Krista's schedule was open until her ten o'clock session with Will, she'd offered to watch the triplets while Gina went to the dentist first thing this morning. In return, Gina would drop Tommy off at school.

The next few minutes were a flurry of activity as three bonnets were removed and three toddlers scampered around the kitchen, then darted into the next room, three pastel streaks of lace, ribbons and perpetual motion.

Krista, Tommy and Gina all poked their heads into the living room where the triplets began pulling Tommy's old baby toys from a cardboard box. Other than Tommy, Gina's twenty-two-month-old girls, Sarah, Beth and Abby, were the most adorable children Krista had ever seen.

"Did I really used to play with those toys?" Tommy whispered.

"You sure did," Krista answered, smoothing her fingers over a stubborn lock of hair near the back of her son's head. The instant she lifted her fingers, the hairs sprang up again.

"Wow," Tommy whispered in awe. "Three babies at once. That is so cool."

Cool was Tommy's favorite word.

"Tommy," Krista said. "Have you brushed your teeth?"

The boy nodded. "I just have to get my backpack and I'll be ready to go."

Instead of turning toward his bedroom, he looked up at Gina and said, "Did you know that only one out of every nine thousand, two hundred and seventy-three babies born is a triplet?"

Gina and Krista exchanged a smile before Gina answered, "No, Tommy, I didn't know that."

"I saw this really long equation in the *Professor's Book of Formulas* at the library the other day, and the librarian said that's what it meant. I thought it was cool and I thought you might want to know." With that, he hurried toward his bedroom, those few stubborn hairs on the very top of his head swaying to and fro with every step he took.

Leaning toward Krista, Gina whispered, "I don't think that professor figured Taylor's stamina into that equation, do you?"

Krista shook her head and rolled her eyes. Ever since her best friend had met and married Taylor Harris, little innuendos about sex had become commonplace.

"I doubt they could have figured in your stamina, either, Gina. Now, why don't you tell me what the girls are going to need while you're gone."

She listened intently as Gina listed everything the triplets might require, from the location of diapers and a change of clothes to the crackers and apple juice she removed from the bag on the counter. Krista wasn't aware of anything amiss, but halfway through, Gina stopped talking and eyed her critically.

"What?" Krista asked.

"It just occurred to me that you're in an awfully good mood this morning and the coffee isn't even on." Without another word, Gina strode across the kitchen and inspected a used mug.

"There are two mugs here, and I happen to know that Tommy is allergic to chocolate," Gina said shrewdly.

"Oh, that one's Will's."

"Will?"

"Will Sutherland."

"You mean a *man* was here?" Gina asked, her voice rising an octave.

"Yes," Krista answered. "But not the way you're thinking."

"How do you know what I'm thinking?"

"Because I know you. Ever since you met Taylor, you've had an X-rated mind."

Gina smiled and pushed her chin-length blond hair out of her face. "Maybe you're the one with the X-rated mind, Krista."

Will had said something similar last night. For heaven's sakes, was it really that obvious?

Even now she was a bit surprised by the ease with which she and Will had talked last night. After eight years, she would have thought they'd be a little uncomfortable with each other. She had no intention of allowing their relationship to go beyond patient-therapist-friend, but she had enjoyed his company.

He'd looked tired when he'd left. Why wouldn't he? He'd driven across two states, settled into a new apartment and had begun a new therapy program. He'd always had incredible stamina, but his fatigue, along with the fact that he'd confided in her about what *didn't* happen between him and his former therapist, made her feelings toward him shift, swell, soften. She'd gone to bed humming last night, and she woke up the same way. For the first time in years, she hadn't needed a cup of coffee to clear her mind and begin a new day.

"Krista, I don't think I've ever seen so many sparks in your eyes," Gina declared.

"These are sparks of battle," she said. "I'm a little surprised by them myself."

"This guy must really be sexy to have you in this good a mood first thing in the morning."

"For heaven's sakes, Gina. Our children are in the next room." Krista glanced around. Finding the coast clear, she smiled grudgingly and said, "As a matter of fact, he is. But I'm not going to give in to the attraction. Forewarned is forearmed."

"I don't know," Gina declared. "Maybe you should give another man a chance."

Krista didn't mind Gina's candor. These conversations were as natural to them as the friendship they'd formed five years ago. Caring people made the world go round. They also made life worth living. Besides, Krista enjoyed teasing Gina just as much.

The voice of a singing dinosaur carried to their ears. Evidently, Tommy had turned the television on for the girls.

"I think you're excited about this guy," Gina insisted.

"Invigorated is more like it."

"Oh, this is wonderful. There's nothing a man likes more than a challenging, invigorated woman."

Even though Krista recognized the teasing tone in Gina's voice, her words were a little disturbing. Will had turned away rather suddenly when he'd left last night. Did he think of her as a challenge? Slowly, she glanced at the empty coffeemaker next to the sink.

"Are you going to introduce me to him sometime?"

"You already know him. Sort of."

"I do?" Gina asked.

"Well, I told you about him once, a long time ago. And you've seen his picture on the cover of the tabloids in the grocery store. He's one of the reasons I swore off men."

"I don't remember seeing anybody named Will on the cover of the tabloids."

"The press doesn't call him Will. To them, he's Billy. Billy the Kid."

Gina's eyes widened as she said, "You mean the Will you used to love and the Will who was here last night is Billy the Kid, the famous baseball player?"

Krista shrugged and slowly nodded, her gaze straying to the empty coffeepot a second time.

"That's who you're having X-rated thoughts about?" Gina asked.

"I never said I was having X-rated thoughts." At least she'd never said it out loud.

"What are X-rated thoughts, Mommy?"

Krista and Gina both turned at the sound of Tommy's voice. The dark-haired waif stood in the kitchen doorway, his backpack in his arms, curiosity in his round brown eyes.

Krista, who had learned to think on her feet where Tommy's questions were concerned, said, "There are all kinds of thoughts. Baby thoughts, happy thoughts, scared thoughts, children and adult thoughts. X-rated thoughts are the kind of thoughts that some adults have sometimes."

"Oh, cool."

Shaking her head at Gina's sardonic grin, Krista turned her attention to Tommy. She wasn't sure she was happy that her son thought it was *cool* to have X-rated thoughts, but she breathed a sigh of relief that he was satisfied with her answer.

"Did you get your math book?"

"Yup. It's in my backpack. Too bad I have to go to school. If I could stay home, I'd help the babies write a letter to Santa Claus."

As bright as Tommy was, he never wanted to go to school. He said the other little boys teased him. It broke Krista's heart, but there wasn't a thing she could do about it.

"It's a little early to be writing letters to Santa, isn't it?" Gina asked.

Tommy shook his head seriously. "Uh-uh. Me and Stephanie—I mean, Stephanie and I already wrote ours."

"You did?" Krista asked. "What did you ask for?"

"It's a secret, and Santa told Stephanie that he works extra hard to make secret wishes come true."

"Santa *told* Stephanie that?" Krista asked. Silently, she thanked God for Tommy's new little friend. Maybe he hadn't become close with any other boys, but he had made friends with a darling little girl. Time, she thought to herself. Give him time.

Tommy nodded. "Do you know what Santa's real name is?"

"Saint Nick?" Krista asked, catching Gina's wink.

With a vigorous shake of his head, Tommy said, "No. You got the first name right. But his last name is Abernathy. Nicholas Abernathy."

Nicholas Abernathy?

The triplets toddled into the kitchen. Amid the flurry of bye-byes and kisses, Krista didn't have the opportunity to ask Tommy how he'd come to know *Santa's* last name. After shooing her friend and son out the back door, she watched as Gina smoothed her fingers along Tommy's little rooster tail. As always, it sprang right back up the instant she removed her hand.

Without warning, Tommy turned and said, "Are you having an X-rated thought right now?"

"No, honey, I'm not."

"Oh," Tommy said, skipping down the sidewalk toward Gina's minivan.

"Too bad," Gina said softly, a mischievous glint in her eyes.

Krista closed the door without answering but that didn't stop Gina's laughter from carrying to her ears. Pouring apple juice into three brightly colored cups with special spouts for sipping, Krista wondered where she would be the next time Tommy brought up the subject of X-rated thoughts.

Now that she thought about it, both Tommy and Will had been inordinately interested in the topic of X-rated thoughts and dirty minds. Krista decided it must be their male hormones, and fleetingly wondered if thinking about male hormones would be considered X-rated.

While the little girls drank their juice, she walked to the counter and started a pot of coffee.

"That's it, Will. Keep your back nice and straight," Krista said.

Sweat trickled down the side of his face, and the muscles in his arms bulged from exertion. Krista grasped the safety belt around his waist with both hands, slowly making her way with him toward the opposite end of the parallel bars.

"Hey, Billy," Brody called on his way by with his own patient. "Lookin' good, man."

She saw Will's chest heave as he sucked in a deep breath. Eyeing the distance to the end, she tried to gauge the amount of energy he had left. Her own arms were tired from holding him steady and from trying to relieve his arms of some of his weight; he must have been exhausted.

"Brody's right, Will. You're doing great."

"Swell."

He'd spoken without breaking the rhythm of his slide-grip-breathe movements as he made his way along the parallel bars. She noticed another bead of sweat roll down his neck.

It had been this way all week. After he'd left her house Tuesday night, she'd thought they were going to be friends. She'd pondered their relationship over coffee while she'd watched Gina's triplets, but all the coffee in Brazil wouldn't help her understand why he'd shown up for his therapy session later that morning with a chip the size of the Liberty Bell on his shoulder.

She'd seen children and adults alike break down and cry from the pain and frustration of trying to force their muscles to work again. The only kind of tears Will shed were tears of sweat. His therapy was grueling, but he never so much as complained.

He'd started hanging around the rehab center, showing up early, eating his lunch in the patient lounge where he and Brody and some of the others had taken to playing poker. He was on a first-name basis with practically everyone on the entire floor, but he barely spoke to her unless it was absolutely unavoidable.

He reached the end of the parallel bars and let out a shuddering breath. Krista knew she shouldn't have been surprised when he moved to turn around and try it again.

"You have to rest for a few minutes," she said sternly.

"I can make it."

"Will, you're pushing yourself too hard," she said, her voice gaining volume. "You could hurt yourself."

"I'll be the judge of that," he barked back.

"Your arms are shaking, your breathing is ragged and you're sweating bullets. I said you have to rest."

"Would you stop treating me like I'm twelve? I said I can make it, dammit, and I will."

"If you two lovebirds could stop arguing for a minute, I have a suggestion."

Krista and Will both turned their heads and glared at Brody. Brody only grinned.

"Would you please tell this...this bullheaded baseball player that even God rested on the seventh day?" Krista said tersely.

She heard Will let out another long shuddering breath, but he still grasped the rails with both hands, and he still hadn't lowered himself into the wheelchair at his knees.

"I'm pretty sure he heard you himself, Krista," Brody said with a chuckle.

"I'm glad someone is finding this funny," she returned. "We therapists usually have to coddle, persuade, even get angry and yell now and then to get our patients to do these exercises. Will here is the first patient I've ever had who tells *me* how to do my job."

"It looks to me as if whatever you're doing is working," Brody replied. "Besides, you sound plenty angry right now yourself."

"Anger beats the hell out of pity."

Will had spoken in a hoarse whisper, but the intensity glittering in his eyes was impossible to miss. Pity? What did he mean anger beats the hell out of pity? If she could have taken her hands from his safety belt, she would have dropped her head into them in exasperation.

"What's your suggestion, Brody?" she finally asked.

"It looks like Will is determined to keep up this grueling pace. Since you think he's pushing himself too hard, why not move his therapy to the pool for the rest of today's session? The buoyancy of the water would take most of the weight off his legs, but he could still work on increasing the strength and movement in his muscles."

"The swimming pool?" Will asked.

"Yeah," Brody answered. "Can you swim?"

Will lowered himself into the wheelchair, landing in the seat the same instant he said, "Yeah, I can swim."

"Does this mean you want to try the pool?" Krista asked.

He cast a sideways glance at Brody before turning his full attention to Krista. When he'd first left her place Tuesday night, he'd cursed her sensitivity, her depth of feeling, her sympathy for his paralysis. After that, he'd cursed his unresponsive leg muscles and his weakness.

"What do you say, Will?" Brody asked, drawing him from his thoughts. "Want to try the pool another time?"

Will eyed the other therapist. Brody Calhoun was built more like a Chippendale dancer than a physical therapist, but his handshake was firm and he seemed honest. The two men had struck up a friendship. Moving his therapy to the pool suddenly sounded like a good idea.

"Well?" Brody insisted.

Casting Krista a sidelong glance, Will said, "And pass up the opportunity to see Krista in a bikini?"

Brody's deep chuckle resounded from one end of the room to the other. "Krista," he said, turning his head slightly. "I think you might have met your match."

"That'll be the day," she sputtered.

Grasping the handles on his wheelchair, she pulled Will around, saying, "Come on. We'll try the pool. If we're lucky, neither one of us will drown."

Will caught Brody's good-humored wink and nodded in return. If he was lucky Krista would continue his therapy in a little black bikini so tiny it could fit in the palm of his right hand. And if he was really lucky, she'd realize that the last thing he wanted was her pity.

Her swimsuit was black. But it wasn't a bikini. It wasn't even two pieces. All in all, it covered her body well. And what a body.

Will was sitting in a wheelchair, watching as she emerged from the dressing room on the other side of the pool. She was naturally dark complected, her skin smooth-looking and healthy. Her hair was still in the French braid she always wore for work. Even from this distance, her eyes glittered darkly in her face. Her chin was at a proud angle, her shoulders even more so. There were muscles in her upper arms, and her breasts were lush and round beneath the suit. Her waist was narrow, as were her hips. His gaze had gotten as far as her upper thighs by the time she reached him.

"Are you ready?" she asked, her glance sweeping over him as she cast him that questioning look he'd seen her use a hundred times this week.

"The question is, are you?" he returned.

His suit was black, too. It wasn't exactly skimpy, but it was made out of stretchy material that left little to the imagination.

"Here, Will," she said, pushing his chair toward the lift at one end of the small swimming pool. "Swing yourself onto this seat. It pivots over the water. After you're strapped on, I'll hop into the water. We can lower you in from there."

Will did as she instructed. Within minutes, he felt the chlorinated water lap at his feet, up his ankles, over his knees. He sucked in a deep, audible breath as the water slowly covered his waist.

He glanced at her face and caught her smiling tentatively at his sharp intake of breath. When she smiled that way, it wasn't easy to stay mad at her. "Come on, get me out of this thing. I'm going to swim," he said, groping for the buckle that would release him from the lift.

She moved his hands aside, deftly unfastening the strap. "Will," she said, her eyes trained on her hands. "You haven't been in a swimming pool since your accident. You're making incredible progress, but you still don't have a lot of strength in your legs. I want this to be a good experience for you, but you have to promise me you'll do as I say."

He took both her hands in his just as the buckle gave way. "I didn't know you cared."

She was standing close to him, their faces nearly level. He didn't know she cared? Sometimes, when she looked into his eyes, she was afraid she cared too much. How could she tell him that? He was staring back at her in silence, waiting. In that instant she realized that even though she didn't know what had come over him this week, he wasn't going to do anything foolish today.

The pool was in a large room with windows along one entire wall. From her position, she saw an orderly amble down the hall. Otherwise, she and Will were completely alone. She pulled her hands from his and spread her arms, moving them in a half circle away from her. "You have the whole pool to yourself. Why don't you see what you can do?"

Will slid from the lift. He'd always had a strong leg kick and it wasn't as easy to move through the water without it. He went under a couple of times, but he always came up again, his arms pulling him through the water. His upper body was strong, and the water was deliciously soft and buoyant. He glided to his side like a seal, floating on his back. Turning to his other side, he let out a loud whoop.

Everything was right with the world. He couldn't remember the last time he'd felt such uncontrollable joy. He was moving on his own. He was free. Suddenly, all his worries, his pain and his frustration faded. Even his disappointment over seeing sympathy in Krista's eyes retreated to some far corner of his mind.

"How are you doing?" Krista asked.

"Come here and I'll show you."

"Will."

They had both reached the side of the pool, both raising a hand to steady themselves by the edge. "This is the best therapy I could have had today, Krista. In fact, this is the best I've felt in years. Why don't we both shimmy out of these swimsuits and make this the best day of our lives?"

She watched a droplet of water run down his face, skimming past his boyishly pouty lips. "In your dreams," she said as casually as she could manage.

"What would you say if I told you that I *have* dreamed of making love with you?" he asked on a husky whisper.

"I'd say you've done a remarkable job of covering it up this week. I've lost track of how many times you've practically bitten my head off. I'd also say that it's perfectly nor mal to have those kind of thoughts about your therapist. It happens all the time, like a woman who's attracted to her doctor, or a student to his teacher. Besides, after all this time, I'm afraid I'm awfully rusty," she added, trying for a light tone.

"I'd do everything I could to make it good for you, to give you pleasure every way I know how."

Her knees felt weakened by the images his words evoked. There was an invitation in the smoldering depths of his blue eyes, one she had to fight not to accept. What was going on with him? She'd heard of mood swings, but this was ridiculous.

"You're too kind," she said, moving away from him slightly.

"This is the first time I've ever been accused of that one," he declared.

"I'm not surprised," she replied.

He was looking at her, his expression completely serious. His eyebrows were lowered slightly, his mouth set in a firm line. He had a well-defined jaw and a decidedly stubborn chin. Even dripping wet, his hair was slightly askew in the front. That little imperfection made her smile.

"What?" he asked.

"Oh, it's nothing. I was just thinking that you really can be sweet."

It was all Will could do not to scowl. He didn't want to look sweet, he wanted to look virile, sexy, damned near irresistible. The way Krista looked to him.

Wet, her hair was nearly black. Droplets of water clung to her eyelashes, others to her cheeks and neck. They were both holding on to the side of the pool. Here, the water only came to the bottom of his ribs, but it hovered just below Krista's armpits, the buoyancy of the water lifting her breasts toward the surface.

He thought she was the hottest thing he'd ever seen, and she thought he was sweet. Wasn't that just great.

"Are you ready for more therapy?" she asked.

He nodded halfheartedly.

"Okay, Will. Back up until your shoulders are flush with the pool wall."

He did as she instructed.

"Now, keep your arms stretched out, resting lightly along the rim of the pool. That's it. Can you feel your weight on your feet?"

Will nodded, his amazement growing.

"Spread your legs out a little so your weight is more evenly distributed."

She was standing directly in front of him, her hands ready to steady him if he should begin to fall. He concentrated on picking up one leg and inching it over. It moved, until little by little, it was positioned exactly as Krista had instructed.

He focused on every muscle from his thighs all the way down to his feet, marveling that he could feel every one. Slowly, he raised his arms, letting them hover just above the rim of the pool. He leaned forward slightly, his back coming away from the wall.

"Look. No hands. No braces or crutches or hands. Krista, I'm standing on my own two feet!"

The water was as transparent as glass and Will's thoughts were just as clear. In that instant he felt whole again, and he gloried in his triumph. It filled his mind and his chest and his body, making him feel invincible, strong, ultimately masculine. This is what he'd dreamed of and worked toward. Feelings surged inside him, want and hope and desire mingling with his accomplishment, pulsing through him. He leaned back against the pool, all those feelings converging to the very center of him.

Before Krista's eyes, Will's expression turned warm and sensuous. His eyelids slid down, his lips parted and his hands glided to her shoulders, gently pulling her close to his body.

"Will, what do you think you're doing?"

"I think you know what I'm doing."

She felt the strength in his arms, the firmness of his chest, but it was the depth of feeling in his voice that heated her thoughts. She lifted her chin to look up into his eyes. His face angled down and she barely managed to turn her head in time to dodge his kiss. He made a sound deep in his throat, a masculine, passionate, slightly frustrated sound before his lips trailed over her cheekbone to the hollow below her ear.

"I know what you're doing," she whispered. "What I want to know is why."

His lips skimmed across her earlobe, his deep voice rasping across her senses as he said, "Does there have to be a reason? Isn't the fact that it feels so good, so right, enough? I'm whole again, Krista, and you're so beautiful, your skin is so soft, your sighs so..."

She hadn't realized she'd sighed until her breath rushed through her parted lips a second time. She also hadn't realized that the warmth of his wet flesh would be so intoxicating. Fitting her more tightly to his body, he slid both palms down the side of her hips, kneading and touching and drawing a response from deep inside her.

When Brody had first suggested she take Will to the pool for his therapy, she'd hoped that neither she nor Will would drown. Right now, she was drowning in sensation, in this man's touch, in his murmurs and in their shared desire.

She hadn't been this close to a man in years, and she hadn't been touched quite like this since... since Will. Not even Tommy's father had been able to draw this kind of response from her so quickly. That thought echoed through her mind, giving her the strength she needed to push against Will's chest and pull away from him slightly at the same time.

Her eyes darted to the row of windows above them. "Will," she whispered. "Someone could see us. Do you know how humiliated I'd feel if that happened?"

"Do you know how good you make *me* feel?" he asked, covering her breast with one hand.

Her eyelashes fluttered down, and she called herself a fool. "I mean it," she said, her voice barely above a whisper. "If someone walks in, I'll never live it down."

His chest rose and fell as he took a deep breath. The look on his face reminded her of the one he'd worn the moment before he'd left her house Tuesday night.

Stiffly, he finally moved his hand to her shoulder. "You'd feel humiliated to be seen kissing a man who can't walk?"

His question sent a roaring din through Krista's ears. She glanced up at him and found that his eyes had darkened like deep water. Just when she was sure that he was as belligerent and ornery as they came, he asked her an honest, heartwrenching question, one that left him vulnerable.

"Is that what you think?" she asked.

"What should I think?"

She fought down the impulse to press her palm to the muscle working in his jaw. If she touched him, he'd know she wanted his touch in return. If that happened, her life as she knew it, not to mention her reputation at the center, would never be the same again. But she couldn't lie to him. She just wasn't sure how to explain how she felt.

"Will," she said quietly. "Those sighs you mentioned weren't fake. I nearly went up in smoke a minute ago, and I'm soaking wet. The reason I won't make love with you has nothing to do with your crutches. Is that why you've been barking my head off all week?"

"I don't want your pity, Krista."

This was the second time he'd used the word *pity*. Looking up at him, she felt so confused that for a moment she couldn't speak. After what seemed like forever, she finally said, "Empathy is not the same thing as pity, Will. I don't pity you. I'm proud of what you've accomplished. I even admire you for your bullheadedness. And for the record, you're the sexiest man I've ever met, with or without your crutches.''

He watched her for a long time, without moving, without speaking, as if he were searching her face for the truth. When she'd all but given up on his saying anything more, he finally spoke. ''Then I don't understand how you could feel humiliated if someone found you kissing me.''

''All my life I've fallen in love with the wrong men, men who didn't love me as much as I loved them. I've always been very...responsive, but I've never been intimate without being in love. I can't say the same about them. My boyfriend in high school loved to brag. Steven did, too.''

''I never said a word about what we did when we were together,'' Will said quietly.

She tipped her head to one side and cast him a sad smile. ''I know, and I appreciated it. But I've been a fool for love too often. After I had Tommy, I decided I was better off on my own, without a man.''

Will seemed to be trying to absorb her explanation. After a moment of silence, he said, ''I think you're missing out on living.''

She peered up at him. ''I suppose you're welcome to your own opinion.''

After a moment, he grinned at her, a devilish glint lighting his eyes. ''You really think I'm the sexiest man you've ever met?''

Krista rolled her eyes and splashed him. He ducked under the water, coming up several feet away. At only five feet three and a half, Krista could touch the bottom with her toe, but she preferred to tread water.

''It's time to go,'' she called, moving her arms and legs through the water.

''Not yet,'' he returned, turning onto his side.

''What do you mean?'' she asked.

''I know my session is over, but I'm afraid this swimsuit doesn't hide much, and unless you want everyone to know what almost happened between us, it's going to take me a few minutes to...relax. If you know what I mean.''

Krista felt her face heat and automatically put her hands on her cheeks. She sank and came up sputtering. Good grief. If she wasn't careful, she was the one who was going to drown.

Four

Will grasped the side of the pool with both hands. He was exhausted, but he didn't care. How could he care when he'd never felt quite this way? Nothing felt better than this, not stealing second, not even hitting a home run when the bases were loaded. He'd stood today. On his own two feet, without crutches or braces. He'd stood.

His former therapist thought he'd never do it. Oh, he knew he still had a long way to go, but he was going to make it back, all the way back.

"Are you okay?" Krista asked.

Positioning himself onto the chair lift, he took a breath and fastened the belt. He raised his chin and cast her a sheepish grin. "I guess I'm more tired than I realized, but believe me, I'm on my way to being completely okay." After a brief pause, he added, "And I have you to thank for it, Krista."

She took a deep breath, too. Reaching for the button that would raise the lift, she said, "This is my job. Besides, you're the one who did all the work."

Will stopped her hand with his own. "It may be your job, but this is my life you're helping me regain. Besides, I'm not so totally self-absorbed that I don't see how difficult your job is. Especially with patients who badger you as much as I have. I'm sorry for snapping at you this week."

"Don't worry about it. It goes with the territory," she said, finally pressing the button along the edge of the pool.

Will watched her expression as he slowly began to rise out of the water. He'd always liked the way she looked, but he couldn't shake the feeling that there was something different about her smile. Maybe the difference was that it didn't quite reach her eyes.

While Krista climbed out of the pool, he looked at a small group of people on the other side of the windows. They reminded him that this wasn't really a private pool, and that Krista had told him she'd be completely embarrassed if anyone saw them kissing.

"I'm sorry about what almost happened over by that wall, too, Krista. I really do have scruples. I'm afraid I got carried away by the moment, not to mention by the way you look in that swimsuit. I also want you to know that as soon as I'm walking on my own again, I'm going to take you to the best French restaurant I can find."

"I'm going to hold you to that, Will."

He tilted his head, his imagination automatically taking her words out of context. "You can hold me any way you want."

He watched as his meaning seeped into her mind, beyond her irritation, past her defenses. Scruples be damned, he'd been unable to keep from responding to her statement.

Krista stepped from the pool and handed Will a large white towel. Wrapping one around herself, she heard him sk if she was going to eat lunch in the cafeteria. She answered him, but her thoughts were so far away that she was only faintly aware of her own voice. There was just something about this man that wrapped around her like strong arms and a warm smile. He was definitely more serious than he'd been in college, but every now and then his old cockiness resurfaced. He'd been back in her life less than one week and she already felt topsy-turvy.

"Krista, I don't mind telling you that once I'm on my feet again, I wouldn't mind ten minutes alone with your ex-husband. He sounds like a total jerk to me, but since you loved him, there must have been a grain of goodness in him somewhere. I'm not surprised you were the person who saw t."

Krista looked on as Will swung himself into the wheelchair, his innate belief in her inner goodness bringing tears o her eyes. She wondered what he'd say if she told him that she'd fallen for Steven on the rebound from *him*.

"Um, Will?"

Her question drew his gaze. Taking a deep breath, she said, "I appreciate your vote of confidence, but there's something I think you should know. I never married Tommy's father."

He was watching her, a look of surprise on his face. "I couldn't," she said hurriedly. "He was already married. He told me he was divorced. I found out the hard way that being separated and being divorced are two very different things."

Neither of them said a word until they'd reached the door o the men's dressing room. A muscle was working in Will's jaw and he stared straight ahead. Krista wasn't sure what she expected him to say, but she'd hoped he'd say something.

"Are you okay?" she asked.

He placed both hands on the rims of his wheelchair before saying, "Yeah, I'm fine. But I think I'm going to need more than ten minutes alone with that bastard."

"It's over, Will. It's been over for a long time. Forget about it. It's lunchtime. Go ahead and change out of that wet suit. As soon as I'm dressed again, I'll push you back to the main floor."

He seemed deep in thought. "Thanks for the offer," he said. "But my therapy session is cutting into your lunch hour, too. After I change, I'll wheel myself on down to the cafeteria. I'll see you later."

She nodded, hurrying off toward the women's changing room.

"Krista?"

Will's deep voice drew her around.

"I'm glad you told me. About Steven, I mean."

She smiled hesitantly. A moment later she pushed the door open and strode into the small room where she quickly drew one black strap from her shoulder. Catching her reflection in the mirror, she stopped.

At first, she'd taken his silence to heart, certain he now saw her in a different light. But if he was glad that she'd told him, that couldn't be true. For some reason, she was glad she'd told him, too.

He'd apologized for reaching for her in the pool. He'd said that he'd been carried away by the moment. Half joking, he'd also said he'd been carried away by the way she'd looked in this suit. For the first time in years, she looked, really looked, at her own reflection.

Her hair was soaking wet and goose bumps had risen on her arms and legs. She'd never thought the rest of her was all that noteworthy. Much to her embarrassment, she'd developed early. Only after Tommy's birth, when she'd breastfed her child, had she become comfortable with her body. Steven used to tell her she had a Barbie doll figure. It had been a compliment of sorts, she supposed, but she'd always bristled. Why hadn't she bristled when Will had just told her that he'd gotten carried away because of the way she looked in her swimsuit?

Gazing into the reflection of her own brown eyes, she knew the answer. It was because she'd always felt as if Will saw more than full breasts and a narrow waist. She'd always sensed that he liked what he saw on the inside as much as what he saw on the outside. That's what had made his leaving eight years ago so painful, and if she wasn't careful, it was going to make his leaving this time even more so.

She suddenly remembered all the times he'd practically snapped her head off this past week. With a shake of her head, she peeled her wet suit from her body and stepped beneath the warm shower. Lathering her hair and body, she chastised herself for not realizing why he'd been so belligerent.

Without intending to, she'd injured his pride, his sexuality. Of course. She of all people should have known how sensitive men who had been paralyzed were about that. The first thing a person who'd suffered a spinal injury asked was, "Am I going to be able to walk again?" The second thing the men usually asked was, "Am I going to be able to have sex?"

In her eyes, Will's injury didn't detract from his sexuality. She should have realized it would in his. Turning the shower off, she quickly dried with another towel, then pulled on her clothes, vowing to be more careful of his feelings in the future.

Krista peeked inside the employee lounge, looking for Mrs. A. Finding the room empty, she transferred the plant that had been delivered for her friend from her right hand to her left and headed in the opposite direction, wondering where everyone had gone. The raucous laughter coming from the patient game room stopped her footsteps. She did an about-face and followed the discordant sounds of raised voices and friendly bantering to the room at the end of the hall.

"That's it. I fold," Brody grumbled.

"I think you're bluffing, Billy," Mrs. A said to Will.

Mrs. A was playing poker?

Krista inched her way into the room, glancing at all the familiar faces. No wonder the employee lounge and patient exercise room had been deserted. Practically everyone was here.

"I'm in," Heather declared, tossing in her own pretzels.

All eyes in the room were trained on Mrs. A, who was studying her cards. "Has anybody ever told you that you look a lot like Mrs. Santa Claus?" Will asked playfully.

After worrying her bottom lip, the white-haired lady eyed her opponents, then slowly slid two pretzels across the table. "If you're trying to rattle me, it isn't working, Billy. I call."

Will eyed his opponents and said, "I really hate to take all of you people's pretzels, but read 'em and weep." With that he plunked three queens down on the table.

The patients who were looking on laughed; Brody and Heather shook their heads, and Mrs. A said, "Just for that I'm going to make sure that the only thing you find in your stocking this year is a lump of coal."

Feigning a stricken look, he said, "Come on, Mrs. A. I've been nice. Just ask Krista."

Everyone turned to look at her. Shaking her head, Krista said, "Naughty is more like it."

There was a good deal of elbow jabbing as patients and therapists alike recalled how often they'd heard Billy the Kid raise his voice this week. *Naughty* was a pretty good description of the way Will had acted.

Brody leaned back in his chair, his blue eyes in startling contrast to his dark-toned skin. "So, Billy," he said. "Does this mean that you got to first base with Krista?"

"You men have one-track minds," Heather admonished.

"No, we don't," one of the male patients declared. "So did you, Billy?"

Ignoring the willowy redhead and the old coot who had repeated Brody's question, Will looked up at Krista. Not more than half an hour ago she'd told him that she'd be humiliated if her fellow therapists caught her kissing him. He knew she was as strong as nails on the outside, but in that instant, he also knew that she was still just as vulnerable on the inside as she'd always been. Maybe even more.

He cast her a playful wink and grinned wryly at Brody. "I tried, but I'm afraid she tagged me before I'd completed my world-famous slide."

Everyone in the room laughed, and everyone offered Will their condolences, saying, "Don't take it to heart."

"Yeah, bigger men than you have struck out with our Krista."

"You try to throw her a curve and she throws you a knuckle ball."

Heather pushed herself away from the round table. "Baseball metaphors. How quaint. Krista, how in the world do you stand this?"

Krista shrugged at her fellow therapist. "Is it any wonder I've become a man-hater? But don't worry, Heather. Will's just feeling his oats because he stood today."

There were gasps and oohs and congratulations all around. Will hardly noticed. He was too busy noticing Krista. The last time he'd seen her, her hair had been soaking wet; so had the rest of her. Now she was wearing a white uniform like the ones she always wore, but her face looked freshly scrubbed, and instead of the usual French braid, her hair was loosely clasped with a wide band partway down her back. She looked utterly soft, wholesome yet delicate. Will had never wanted her more.

He was used to going after what he wanted, with everything he had, no holds barred, full speed ahead. But he couldn't rush in and sweep her off her feet. He couldn't even walk for God's sake. Where did that leave him? All he knew was that he wanted to see her, to spend time with her, to get

to know her all over again. He didn't have a clue how he was
going to do that.

Krista listened to the playful bantering throughout the
room. Will appeared strong willed and brashly self-
confident. No one else seemed to see the sweetness inside
him. He could have bragged about touching her in the pool.
Guys in her past who hadn't gotten half as far as Will sure
had. He was respecting her wish for privacy. The knowledge brought with it an innate sense of wonder.

"Well," Heather said, standing. "I have some paper-
work to do before my next patient arrives, so I'm out of the
game. Krista, why don't you take my place?"

Brody grumbled that changing players halfway through
a game was unfair, and Will said, "What are you com-
plaining about? If I win, Krista will probably take it out on
me in therapy."

Lowering into her seat, Krista placed the plant she'd carried into the room in front of Mrs. A. "This came for you,"
she told her sprightly friend.

Eyeing Will, the first player on her left, Krista said, "And
that last statement is going to cost you."

He slanted her a decadent look and replied, "You
wouldn't believe how much I'm looking forward to paying
up."

"Put your money where your mouth is, Will, and deal the
cards," one of the patients insisted.

Will's eyes raked over Krista, stopping in places that
seemed to warm from the heat of his gaze, making her infinitely aware of where he was thinking about putting his
mouth. She glanced around the table. Every person in the
room seemed to be waiting for her reaction.

"Sometimes it's hard *not* to dislike men, don't you agree
Mrs. A?" she asked.

The older woman blinked rapidly as she held up a beautiful violet in full bloom. "It's harder not to love them," she
said softly.

Every man in the room puffed up his chest, wholeheartedly agreeing that they were indeed hard *not* to love.

"Your plant is beautiful," Krista said. "Who's it from?"

The look on Mrs. A's face mingled pride and tenderness as she said, "It's from my husband."

"I'm glad," Krista said softly. Most of the people in the room knew that Mrs. A's husband was out of the country on business. What the rest of them didn't know was that he hadn't wanted her to take this job here in Allentown. If the blooming violet was an accurate indication, Krista had a feeling the old gentleman was having a change of heart.

"Ah, yes," Mrs. A said quietly, touching a finger to one tiny blossom. "Men are indeed hard not to love."

Casting a sideways glance at Will, Krista was afraid that Mrs. A had been right. Some men were definitely hard not to love.

Will stood outside the glass doors of the patient exercise room, watching Krista. It had been a week since he'd stood for the first time in the pool. A lot had changed in that week. He was regaining some movement in his legs and had kissed his leg braces goodbye. It was amazing how many times the word *kissed* had crept into his thoughts. Every time it did, the image of Krista's dark eyes and kiss-swollen lips shimmered across his mind.

He was thrilled that he didn't need the braces, but the biggest change was in his relationship with Krista. Outwardly, things were much the same. He still pushed himself beyond his limits and she still issued commands. He still teased her and she still told him to can it every now and then. But underneath their bantering, there was a new level of understanding and, on his part at least, a new sense of amazement.

Yesterday, he'd seen her with an elderly patient who'd recently suffered a stroke. The man was making remarkable progress and had a wonderful outlook, not to mention a fine mind and a rather seedy sense of humor.

"Come on, Krista," he'd said, slurring his words slightly. "When are you going to break your vow of celibacy and run away with me?"

Moving at his side next to his walker, she'd said, "You know I would, Mr. Crenshaw, if I hadn't made that bothersome vow to myself."

Will was stupefied. Did everyone know she'd sworn off men?

She claimed she was a man-hater, but there wasn't a man on the entire floor who believed her. She'd always been a little embarrassed about her sexuality, yet everyone in the rehab center seemed to agree that she was one of the most sensuous women they'd ever known. Brody teased her about her *vow*, and more than one patient had offered themselves up for such a *worthy* cause.

Will might have understood why she didn't take them up on their offers if she'd done it for moral reasons. He also knew that in this day and age a person couldn't be too careful. But Krista hadn't given up on men for either of those reasons. She said she'd done it to find her own happiness. But she wasn't happy, at least not the way she deserved to be. He couldn't put his finger on how he knew. She was so warm and vibrant and had so much to give. Why wasn't she looking for a loving relationship?

She'd told him that the men in her life used to brag about her. He knew that some women wouldn't be fazed by such a thing, but Krista's ego had been battered by her sisters and by the men she'd loved. Still, no matter what she said about not needing or wanting a man, Will happened to know that there were passionate embers deep inside her. He wanted to fan them, watch them turn into a red-hot inferno.

"She's something else, isn't she?"

Will glanced behind him at the sound of Mrs. A's voice. Nodding, he turned his attention back to Krista. She was leaning over a young girl of ten or eleven who was trying to learn how to walk with the use of a prosthetic leg. He'd seen the little girl break down and sob twice already. It was all Will could do to watch.

"I don't know how Krista does it," he said to Mrs. A. "I mean, it's no wonder she has to relieve her stress on the treadmill at the end of the day. Her pace is exhausting and that little girl's story is heartbreaking. Yet Krista never lets on."

"She's a remarkable woman, all right. But she lets on. She's talked to me about it, so I know sometimes, late at night, all alone in the dark, she lets on."

A heaviness centered in Will's chest at the thought of Krista sitting all alone in the dark, thinking and worrying and hurting, with no one to hold her. "Her life appears to be full and rewarding," he said quietly.

"Ah, yes, it is that," Mrs. A agreed, her blue eyes twinkling. "I've been here for two months, and everybody just loves her to pieces. She has many friends, and of course she adores her little boy. He's a handful, that one is. Smart as a whip, wily as a sailor, but sweet as honey. Just like Krista was at that age. Only Krista never had anyone who appreciated her particular kind of gift, and she never asked for a baseball glove for Christmas. Seems to me she wanted a horse. Unfortunately, horses don't fit in sleighs. Land sakes, just look at the time. I have to go. Talk to you later, Billy."

Will felt his mouth drop open. What did Mrs. A mean "horses don't fit in sleighs"? He thought about following her and asking, but the older lady had swept down the hall as if she had wings on her feet, and Will doubted he'd ever be able to catch her.

A faint, melodious sound carried to his ears. He glanced all around him, only to find that the corridor was deserted. Strange. He thought he'd heard sleigh bells.

Sleigh bells? It was only October, for heaven's sake. Looking straight ahead, he fleetingly wondered if maybe

Krista had been right. Maybe he *was* pushing himself too hard.

She chose that moment to glance up, her gaze meeting his through the thick glass. She said something to the child and a heartbeat later, the little girl waved shyly, her tears forgotten. Krista smiled, too, and Will felt as if the wind had been knocked out of him. He returned the girl's wave and did his best to return Krista's smile. Something intense filtered through his entrancement. This wasn't just a simple case of him wanting a woman. There was more to it than that. Will didn't know what, exactly, but he did know that he'd never felt quite this way. And he knew that it all had something to do with Krista, and the way her smiles didn't quite reach her eyes.

"Here, Billy! Catch."

Will looked up in the nick of time, catching the airborne can of beer before it could hit the wall behind him.

"You haven't lost your touch, Billy," Joe Salez, the team's star pitcher said, wiggling his bushy brows and smiling beneath his thick mustache.

"Yeah," Arnie Beltula, their shortstop, agreed. "Hey, Billy, do you remember that catch you made in the game against the Red Sox? Ninth inning, bases loaded, batter hits a pop-up fly right over third base. I swear you jumped four feet straight in the air to catch that ball."

Will placed the unopened beer can on the table next to the half-eaten pizza and smoking ashtrays. Nodding, he said, "How could I forget? That was the same game that Danny Boy hit his first home run of the season. Remember that Danny?"

The guys fell for the bait, talking among themselves, retelling the details of that ball game until it had reached fish-story proportions. Will breathed a secret sigh of relief. His friends had shown up at his door two hours ago, grinning from ear to ear, carrying coolers and pizza, and so full of bull that Will had laughed out loud.

God, it was great to see them. Truly great.

"There!" Joe said, lunging for the remote control. "You guys gotta see this pitch in slow motion."

"We've seen that pitch in slow motion eighteen times," Danny Boy grumbled around a bite of pizza.

Arnie slammed his fist against the end table, and Joe let out a loud whoop. Will peered through the gray cloud of smoke filling the room at the baseball game playing on the VCR and then at the other three men gathered in his living room.

The four of them had been inseparable for the past three years. These were the guys, his teammates, his family six months out of the year. It was great to see them. Truly... great.

He wondered what Krista was doing.

"Was that some game, or what?" Danny Boy asked when the video had ended, his words starting to slur slightly.

Everybody agreed that it was some game.

"Hey," Arnie said. "What do you say we move this party to the local bar. Maybe play a few games of pool, maybe check out the local women..."

Joe and Danny Boy jumped to their feet, eager to party. Will eyed his three best friends, wishing for a fraction of their enthusiasm. There was only one local woman Will wanted to see, and he highly doubted that she spent her Friday nights in pool halls or bars.

Reaching for his crutches, he found his feet and said, "You guys go ahead. I'm beat."

"Come on, Billy," Arnie cajoled. "It wouldn't be a party without you."

"If you want to stay here, we don't have to move the party," Danny Boy assured him.

"Yeah, it's enough that we're all together again," Joe added.

"I appreciate it, guys," Will said. "But I really am beat. My physical therapy is a helluva lot of work. Did I tell you that I've been swimming as part of my therapy? My leg braces are history. And I've been standing on my own, too."

The back slaps nearly knocked him over. "You're gonna be back with the team in no time!" Arnie shouted.

"Yeah," Joe added. "It'll be just like old times. On the road, practicing until you hurt, then playing ball with everything you've got.

"Then going out on the town every chance we get," Danny said, rubbing his hands together with a flourish.

"That sounds great," Will said quietly, wondering why his voice sounded so hollow. He must have been more tired than he realized. Why else would he be feeling so far removed from his friends?

He'd felt as if the walls in his apartment had been closing in on him for the past two weeks. It had been too quiet. He'd been too alone. The room wasn't lonely or quiet right now. So why was he almost looking forward to the guys' leaving?

"So," Arnie asked, "what do you want to do now?"

"Let's watch my sucker pitch again," Joe insisted, already reaching for the remote.

"If I have to watch that sucker pitch one more time I'm going to show you my sucker pitch," Arnie promised, making a fist.

"No need to get huffy," Joe crowed.

"That's what you think," Arnie snapped.

"Guys," Will said, intervening. "I appreciate the offer, but I really am beat. How about a rain check?"

"Anytime," Danny Boy said.

"Are you sure?" Arnie asked. At Will's nod, he shrugged and reached for a cooler.

Grabbing another slice of pizza, Joe said, "We're going to be in town until Sunday. We'll have the rest of the weekend together."

"That sounds...great," Will declared. It suddenly looked as if it was going to be a long weekend.

"It's so good to see you, Billy," Joe and Danny Boy said, not quite at the same time.

"It's good to see you, too."

Great.

"I've got at least a dozen more tapes to show you," Joe insisted.

Danny and Arnie both groaned, and Will closed the door on the argument that ensued. *A dozen more tapes?* It was definitely going to be a long, long weekend.

He spent the next fifteen minutes traipsing from the living room to the kitchen, carrying used beer cans and paper plates to the trash, emptying ashtrays and restoring a general sense of order to his nondescript apartment. He opened the window a crack, hoping to clear out some of the cigarette smoke, and looked around. The apartment was in a high-rent district. Maybe it wasn't the apartment that was nondescript. Maybe it was his mood.

It was only nine-thirty. He hadn't lied when he'd told the guys he was tired. He just hadn't bothered telling them that he was too keyed up to sleep. Evidently he hadn't let on, because they hadn't noticed. That reminded him of the conversation he'd had with Mrs. A earlier today, when she'd said that Krista "let on" when she was all alone in the dark. Will knew what it was like to be alone in the dark.

Standing in front of the bathroom mirror, he ran a hand through his hair and watched it settle every which way, thinking about how gentle Krista had been with that little girl today, thinking about her unfailing spirit, her sense of humor and her inner strength.

He pulled a comb through his hair and brushed his teeth, wondering if Krista was lonely tonight. Moving his palm across the stubble on his chin, he thought about shaving, then watched his reflection smile.

How long had it been since he'd wanted to impress a woman? He happened to know that Krista wasn't easily impressed. It would take a lot more than shaving to do that. As he thought of her, his smile broadened. Maybe it wouldn't be such a long weekend, after all.

He flipped off the light and proceeded on through the apartment. The baseball glove lying on the arm of the couch reminded him of something else Mrs. A had told him this afternoon, something about baseball gloves and horses and wily sailors. The rest didn't make much sense to him, but the part about a little boy wanting a baseball mitt hit home. When he was Tommy's age, he'd asked for the same thing. Will tucked the glove underneath his arm and headed for the door, wondering if six-year-old boys who were gifted stayed up past nine-thirty on Friday nights.

For the second time that week, he put his crutches in his car and drove through the hilly streets of Allentown then pulled onto Highway 309 and headed for Coopersburg. Long before he reached the village limits, he felt another smile steal across his mouth. Half an hour ago he'd been tired to the bone. He wasn't tired anymore. Will Sutherland had gotten his second wind.

"What does Santa Claus really look like?" Tommy whispered.

The little boy watched, mesmerized, as Stephanie Harris's eyes glowed with excitement. "He doesn't really wear a red coat and black boots, but he has a curly white beard and the nicest blue eyes you'll ever see."

"When he laughs, does his belly really shake like a bowl full of jelly?"

Stephanie nodded and giggled behind her hand. "He says it's from all the cookies boys and girls leave him on Christmas Eve."

"Cool," Tommy whispered.

He peered around Stephanie. Hearing the tell-tale sounds of his mother pouring popcorn into a pan, he knew that he and Stephanie had a few more minutes to talk. "Have you told anybody else that the real Santa Claus used to live in your apartment building when you lived in Quakertown?"

"I told Amy Jo Parker, but she didn't believe me, and I told my little brother, but he's only two and he believes everything I tell him. You're the only friend I have who really believes."

Tommy could read at a fifth-grade level and already understood the beginning concepts of algebra, but he didn't have any idea why he suddenly felt like puffing up his chest and grinning from ear to ear. All he knew was that it felt good—really, really good.

"Do you think he got my letter?" he asked.

"Of course he did. Santa gets all his letters," she said matter-of-factly.

"I wish I would have sent it registered mail so I could be sure," he said.

"You don't need a registered letter, Tommy," Stephanie insisted. "All you need to do is believe."

Tommy felt his face brighten. "Really? Is that why you got your father two years ago?"

Stephanie nodded gravely. "I believed with my whole heart."

Tommy closed his eyes and wished with everything he had. "I believe I'll get a baseball glove and a dog and a father. Especially a father. I really and truly believe."

"Good," Stephanie said. "Now, be on the lookout for a man with white hair and twinkling blue eyes. If you see him, your wishes are bound to come true."

"I'll be on the lookout," Tommy promised. "Oh, I wish Christmas would hurry up and arrive."

"I know," Stephanie agreed. "The waiting is the hardest part. Mr. Abernathy always told me that waiting was also half the fun."

"I don't know, Stephanie," Tommy said, shaking his head slowly. "I hate to wait. I wish that Santa Claus would just come right over and knock on my door."

"Me too," she said with a giggle. "Me too."

The sound of a large fist rapping on the front door drew their attention. Tommy jumped to his feet then stood there as if frozen to the spot. When the knock came again, he looked at Stephanie. Her eyes were open wide and a smile of wonder pulled at her lips.

"Do you suppose that could be Santa Claus?" she whispered.

"Oh, Stephanie, wouldn't that be cool?"

Five

Was that a knock on the door? Krista strained her ears, trying to listen over the sounds of popping corn and the children's movie playing on the VCR.

"I'll get it, Mommy!"

"Tommy, wait!" Krista called, pulling the popcorn maker's plug and hurrying into the next room. By the time she got to the living room, the front door was wide open.

"You're not Santa Claus," Tommy cried.

Krista breathed a sigh of relief that the children hadn't opened the door to an ax murderer. Looking from one child to the other, it suddenly dawned on her what her son just said. *Santa Claus?*

"Tommy," she said. "Do you remember when I told you not to open any door until you know who's on the other side?"

Tommy looked from her to Will and back again, uncertainty widening his dark eyes. Times like these, she wished she could just pull her son into her arms and pretend that nothing bad could ever happen. She didn't want to shatter his trust in adults, yet she knew she had to instill a tiny bit of caution in him.

"My mommy won't let me open the door, either, Tommy," Stephanie said matter-of-factly.

"Why not?" Tommy asked.

"In case the person knocking on the door is a kidnapper," she answered gravely.

Krista met Will's gaze and shook her head. Leave it to a child to make an adult's fears seem unrealistic. Casting the children a wry smile, she thought that Stephanie might have a point. There probably weren't all that many polite ax murderers and kidnappers out there who would knock patiently on a person's door.

"Hello, Will," she said softly.

He smiled, but before he could say anything, Tommy piped up and asked, "Why do you call Billy the Kid Will, Mommy?"

"Because that's his name," she answered. "Like yours is Tom and Tommy and Thomas."

"And because your mom and I are old ... friends," Will added, his deep voice catching on the last word.

Krista didn't miss the appreciative glint in the depths of Will's eyes as he took in her mussed hair and casual knit clothes. It was the same look he'd given her before, lots of times, a look that heated her from the inside.

"Cool," Tommy declared. "Me and Stephanie—I mean, Stephanie and I—are friends, too. What are you doing with that ball glove?"

"Whoa," Krista said. "Let's invite Mr. Sutherland in before we start asking him questions, okay?" To Will, she said, "Would you like to come in?"

"That's a question, Mommy."

Will chuckled out loud. He was beginning to understand what Mrs. A had meant when she'd said that Tommy was as smart as a whip and as wily as a sailor. He'd only been around this little kid for three minutes but he already felt as if he had sea legs.

He settled himself onto the sofa and propped his crutches against the end table. Holding up the glove, he winked at Tommy and said, "I heard you asked for a baseball glove for Christmas. I know this one isn't new, but since it's early, I thought you might settle for one of mine."

Tommy reached for the glove as if it was the Holy Grail. "You really brought this over for me? *Cool.*"

The little girl with wavy brown hair and a faint sprinkling of freckles across her nose looked the glove over carefully. "It smells kind of funny, but it's exactly what you asked for. See? It's a real leather major-league baseball glove. But I thought we were going to keep your Christmas wishes a secret."

The boy stared at the ball glove, dreaminess spilling from his eyes. "I didn't tell, Stephanie. Honest. The only two people I told about my Christmas wishes were you and Santa Claus."

His eyes grew round with wonder as he turned to Will and asked, "Are you Santa's son?"

Will cast a look at Krista. "Santa's son?" he asked.

"Tommy," Krista said softly. "Will's father lives on a ranch in Nebraska, not at the North Pole."

Will eyed the two children who were looking up at him with rapt attention. "That's right," he said seriously. "My dad's hair is turning white, and he's getting quite a paunch from eating Mom's cooking all these years, but he's always home on Christmas Eve."

"Oh," Tommy said, obviously disappointed. "Then how did you know I wanted a baseball glove for Christmas?"

This kid didn't miss a thing. Shrugging, Will said, "Mrs. told me."

Tommy and Stephanie stared at each other.

"Mrs. A," Stephanie said.

"Mrs. A," Tommy repeated. "The *A* probably stands for Abernathy."

"Mr. Abernathy is Mr. Santa Claus," Stephanie insisted.

"So Mrs. A must be Mrs. Santa Claus," they said together, screeching with excitement.

Abernathy? Krista tried to remember where she'd heard that name. "Kids," she said. "I don't think Mrs. A is Mrs. Santa Claus."

"You don't?" Tommy asked, his face falling.

"Well," she stammered. "Um. I suppose anything is possible, but why would Mrs. Santa Claus be working at the Fourth Street Rehab Center?"

Krista never knew just what to say when she was facing this dilemma. She didn't want to lie to her child, nor did she want to dash his belief in Christmas magic. "Tommy, honey," she began. "I'm pretty sure..."

"Don't be too hasty here," Will said, catching her eye. "Mrs. A does have twinkling blue eyes and snow white hair and she did tell me she'd make sure I got a lump of coal in my stocking if I wasn't good."

"I knew it!" Tommy insisted, jumping to his feet. "Now that I got my first wish, I just know I'm going to get the other two wishes, too." His mouth fell open as he looked from his new baseball glove... to Will.

"What other two wishes?" Krista asked softly.

"I can't tell you," Tommy answered solemnly without taking his eyes from Will. "Or they might not come true."

Krista wondered how those wishes were going to come true if she didn't even know what they were. She knew the matter wasn't over for good, but for now at least, Tommy still believed.

"Why don't you three make yourselves comfortable," she said. "And I'll go make a new batch of popcorn."

At the kitchen doorway, she glanced behind her. The sight of Tommy and Stephanie standing between Will's knee slowly drew her around. The kids were listening intently as he showed them how to position the large ball glove on their small hands. A knot rose to her throat, and for a moment she felt wrapped in warmth. Her head automatically tilted to one side; her heart automatically did the same thing.

What was it about this man that made her feel this way? He'd been as ornery as a bear all week, and here she was, thinking he was the most amazing person she'd ever met. It had been over six years since she'd been with a man. Why did the sight of Will showering her son with kindness strike such a vibrant chord inside her?

Was it because he'd changed? Or was it because he hadn't changed completely?

She reminded herself that she wasn't a love-starved young girl anymore. She was a levelheaded, independent woman with a child of her own. Still, there was a tiny ember deep inside her that continued to glow with hope. It was like the last stubborn candle on a birthday cake. No matter how hard she tried, she couldn't blow it out. If she gave in to these feelings flickering through her, she was afraid her heart would get broken all over again.

Striding into the kitchen, she thought about the reason Will had come to the rehab center. He'd done it because he wanted to regain his strength and to learn to walk again. Every step he took would take him farther away from her. Remember that, she told herself as she dumped the soggy popcorn into the trash.

Remember that before you allow romantic notions to fill your mind and heart. Remember? How could she forget?

She measured popcorn into the hot air popcorn maker, thinking about the baseball glove Will had given to Tommy, about how proud Will was each time he made progress in his rehabilitation. Unbidden came the memory of how good it had felt to be held in his arms. It looked as if there were going to be a lot of things she wouldn't be able to forget after Will left again.

From somewhere came the memory of how utterly sad she'd been after he'd left eight years ago. He'd never promised her forever, but his leaving had still rocked her entire world. She'd been so sad, so lonely, so lost. She'd loved him, purely and completely. It had taken a long time to get over him. To this day, she hadn't forgotten. Just as she doubted she'd ever forget the way Tommy had looked at him when Will had given him that ball glove, when Will hadn't dashed her little boy's belief in Christmas.

A series of clunks and thuds alerted her to Will's presence in the room. Turning her back on the humming popcorn maker, she said, "Thanks to you, I'm pretty sure Tommy will be putting carrots out for Rudolph again this Christmas."

When he didn't answer, she followed his gaze to the bay window across the room. Wondering what he was thinking about, she asked, "Were the walls closing in on you again tonight?"

There was only silence.

"Will?"

He looked up with a start. "What? Oh, no, the walls didn't move tonight, although they heard an earful." Raising one corner of his mouth, he said, "Some of the guys from the team are in town this weekend. They stopped by."

"You must have enjoyed that."

"Yeah. It was great."

Krista wondered why he didn't sound more enthusiastic. "If your friends are in town, why are you here?"

"I'm not sure. I guess it had something to do with Tommy, and what you told me about his father. Tell me, Krista. Does Tommy ever see him?"

He'd spoken softly, his voice smooth and deep. It rekindled old feelings deep inside her, old sentiments and emotions she thought she'd forgotten. Now she knew those feelings were still there, shifting and changing and growing whenever she spent time with this man.

He wanted to know about Steven. Maybe it would be best if she told him. Maybe it would chase the interest from his eyes, and the yearning from her heart.

She leaned against the counter, trying to decide where to begin. She dreaded telling the story, dreaded seeing the reproach in Will's eyes. Taking a shallow breath, she finally said, "Steven was an administrator at the rehab center in Philadelphia where I worked after I graduated from college. He was bright and attractive and ten years older than I was. I thought he loved me, and I thought I'd finally found something stable."

"This afternoon you said you didn't know he was married. Did he tell you he was divorced?" Will asked.

She nodded. "And I believed him. I thought he wanted to marry me."

"He didn't?"

"No. He was reconciling with his wife but he didn't want to lose me. He asked me to move to Pittsburgh where he was climbing up the ladder of success."

"You turned him down."

The tone of Will's voice was amazing. What amazed her even more was the fact that he still seemed to believe in her. He didn't chastise her for falling in love with a married man. He seemed to realize that she wouldn't have allowed herself to become involved with Steven if she'd known.

"My relationship with Steven was my biggest mistake. It was also my best, because it gave me Tommy."

The way Krista had said "Steven" grated on his nerves like fingernails on a chalkboard. "Does Tommy know about his father?"

"He's asked a few questions, and someday I'm going to have to tell him, but Tommy's never met his father. Steven thought a child would *complicate* things."

Will swore under his breath. He wouldn't have minded *complicating* a few things in the other man's life. Steven had

a child, a smart, active, handsome little boy. How could he
not care?

Will thought about all the hours he and Cort had spent
with their parents when they were growing up, all the baseball games his family had watched him play, all the wres-
tling matches and water fights and the laughter and the work
they'd done together. Stacking bales of hay had made him
strong; running home over newly plowed fields had made
him one of the fastest base runners in America.

Tommy didn't have both his parents. Yet he was still one
of the luckiest kids in the world because Krista was his
mother, and she'd make sure he grew up strong and secure.

So many things were beginning to make sense to Will.
Krista had been involved with a man she'd worked with. The
gossip must have been terrible. To top it all off, the man
she'd loved hadn't wanted their child.

Men could be such jerks. No wonder she'd sworn off
them.

Her ego had been battered by her three older sisters, and
her heart had been bruised by the men she'd loved. For the
first time, Will realized that *he'd* been one of those men.
He'd hurt her, and then, eight years later, he'd come to her
asking for her help. She could have turned him away, and
yet, she hadn't. Because of her, he'd made remarkable
progress. He wanted to give something back to her. He
wanted to kiss her and touch her. But he also wanted to win
back her belief in men. In him.

Krista didn't know what Will was thinking. His eyebrows were drawn down and his jaw was clenched tight.
Whatever his thoughts were, they must have been intense.

"Will?"

He made a sound deep in his throat, a sound that went
straight to her head. Giving herself a mental shake to clear
her mind, she asked, "Have you decided what your plans
are?"

"My plans?"

She nodded. "Your goals. You know, what you want to do, where you want to go."

He didn't come closer, but as his voice dipped lower, the distance between them seemed to grow shorter. "Right now I'd like to kiss you, and after the kids go to sleep, I'd like to kiss you again. And after that..."

His words trailed away, straight to her imagination. Thoughts shimmered through her mind and whirled across her senses, warming her mind and her body.

"I didn't mean *those* goals," she said hoarsely. "I meant your long-term goals."

He was leaning against the counter, the recessed lighting overhead casting a white glow on his features. His eyes looked deeper, darker and filled with a curious intensity. She felt hypnotized, mesmerized by his expression. Slowly, he made his way across the kitchen, stopping mere inches from her.

Leaning on his crutches, he brought one hand up to her face, trailing his fingertips over her cheekbone, smoothing the back of his hand along her jaw, his gaze homing in on her lips. In a deep and husky tone of voice, he said, "Right now I'd be happy to see you smile."

The sound of his voice and the touch of his hand affected her so deeply that moisture gathered in her eyes. Her heart thudded once, twice, three times. As his face drew closer, her eyelashes fluttered down. He wanted to see her smile, but at that moment, she couldn't have smiled if she'd tried. All she could think about was the warmth in Will's fingertips and the attraction building between them.

The popcorn maker hummed behind her, a perfect match for her thrumming pulse. With her eyes closed, she breathed in the scent of the late-autumn breeze clinging to his clothes. The first brush of his lips was so tender it took her breath away; the second weakened her knees.

He made a sound deep in his throat that only added to her growing desire. She tipped her head slightly, the coarse stubble on his cheek rasping over her skin. A knot rose in her throat; her emotions whirled and her senses reeled. When his hands encircled her upper arms, drawing her closer, the kiss grew more urgent, his mouth more insistent. Responses flickered all across her body, making her yearn for more than this one kiss.

The first kernel of popcorn pinged off the plastic lid, making them both jump. Their lips parted, their eyes opened partway and their breaths came in deep drafts.

Will loosened his hold on Krista's arms and took a step back. The popcorn was popping with a vengeance now, steam rising up behind her. It somehow added to the dreaminess in her eyes, the softness in her expression.

When he finally found his voice, it was as deep as his thoughts. "I'll never be able to smell fresh popcorn without remembering that kiss."

She tucked her lower lip between her teeth, the moisture in her eyes making them look darker and more mysterious. A tiny smile pulled at her lips. "Neither will I, Will. Neither will I."

Will watched as she blinked those tears away. Moments later, he saw that the tiny smile on her lips was reflected in her eyes.

The softening of her features reached inside him, spreading to a place beyond his heart, a place he couldn't name. He felt a curious sense of nostalgia, yet he was certain he'd never felt exactly this way in his entire life.

His heart thudded in his chest and his spirits spiraled upward. He didn't know what was happening to him, but whatever it was, it was invigorating, exhilarating.

"Is the popcorn almost ready?" Tommy called from the living room.

The child's question seemed to jar them both from their thoughts, but Will was the one to answer. "Almost, Tommy."

He let his hands fall away from her arms, but he couldn't help it when one corner of his mouth raised into a speculative grin. When his smile drew up the other side of his mouth, too, her eyes narrowed and he could practically hear her thoughts.

"That shouldn't have happened," she said firmly.

He took another step back, then slowly said, "I think it was meant to happen. I think it's the reason I came here."

Her eyebrows rose a fraction as she asked, "You came over to my house to kiss me?"

He'd meant *here* in a broader sense. Not *here* tonight, but *here* to Pennsylvania and back into Krista's life. He didn't think she was ready to hear that. He wasn't even sure he was ready to say it out loud.

"I wasn't referring to the kiss," he finally said, his voice little more than a husky whisper. "Not that it wasn't pure heaven. I meant your smile. That's what I came here to see."

The tears were back in her eyes again. "That's sweet, Will, but it doesn't change the fact that I am absolutely not going to get involved with you again."

He'd had a feeling she was going to say that. Will wished he knew how to change her mind. He needed a plan. Right now, he needed to buy a little time, so he said, "That's good."

Krista's head jerked up at Will's jaunty tone of voice. She'd expected an argument or at least some provocative comeback. The last thing she'd expected was to have him agree with her. She wondered why she wasn't happier about it and wished she didn't feel the tiniest bit disappointed.

"Since you've made up your mind that you're *absolutely not going to get involved with me*," he continued matter-of-factly, "there should be no reason why we can't go sight-seeing tomorrow afternoon."

For a moment she stood with her mouth open, trying to remember if he'd ever been hit in the head with a line drive, yet feeling as if *she* had been. "Sight-seeing?" she asked inanely.

"Yeah. All I've seen of Pennsylvania is the ball stadium, the rehab center and the inside of my apartment. You seem to love it here. Would you show me what you love? We can take my car. It's the least I can do considering everything you've done for me these past two weeks."

She followed him out to the living room and somehow managed to open the front door. He said goodbye to the kids and cast her a steady look. "I'll call you tomorrow, after you've had a chance to think about it. Good night, Krista."

Before she could say a word, he swung down the steps on his crutches. She stayed where she was in the doorway, watching him make his way over the leaf-strewn sidewalk, wondering why she hadn't simply told him no. Immediately, firmly, adamantly.

"Will's cool, isn't he, Mommy?"

She heard her son's question, but she didn't take her eyes from Will's retreating back. Cool? Warm as a tropical breeze was more like it, a tropical breeze that smoothed over a person's skin like a husky whisper, murmuring praise and bringing pleasure....

"Mommy?"

"Hmm?" she answered.

"Now are you having X-rated thoughts?"

The door closed with a quiet click. Krista glanced over at Stephanie, relieved to find that she was munching popcorn and watching the end of the animated movie, oblivious to Tommy's latest question. If only her son were doing the same thing.

"Are you?" Tommy repeated.

She pressed her fingertips to her kiss-swollen lips, at a loss for words. Finally, she strode to the coffee table and handed her son a bowl. "Just eat your popcorn, okay?" she said, her voice cracking despite her efforts to remain in control.

He cast her another sidelong glance and grinned imp-
ishly before settling himself on the sofa and turning his attention to his favorite movie. Krista popped two pieces of
fluffy white corn into her mouth. For at least the millionth
time since Tommy had been born, she thought that he was
simply too smart for *her* own good.

"Tommy actually asked you if you were having X-rated
thoughts?" Gina asked the next morning, her voice spar-
kling with laughter.

Krista nodded at her friend and poured herself another
cup of coffee.

"What did you say?"

Holding her mug of coffee a few inches from her mouth,
Krista sputtered, "Well, I couldn't lie to him, but I couldn't
very well tell him the truth, either. So I told him to eat his
popcorn. Besides, ever since Will kissed me here in the
kitchen..."

"He really kissed you in the kitchen?"

Placing the nearly full mug on the table in front of her,
Krista said, "Oh, Gina. What am I going to do?"

"That depends. How was it?"

Krista dropped her face into her hands and groaned. "It
was wonderful. That's the problem."

She felt Gina's hand flutter to her arm, the warmth of her
best friend's palm filtering through her panic. "Why don't
you tell me about this problem," Gina said softly.

Krista lowered her hands and glanced out the window into
the backyard where Tommy was tossing a ball into the air
and catching it with his "new" glove. Turning around
again, she finally said, "I'm scared. Will was always a lot of
fun, but he's not an overgrown kid anymore. He's a man.
He's wonderful to Tommy, and he treats the other patients
at the rehab center with genuine respect."

"Why does that scare you?" Gina asked.

"I wasn't sure, until Katrina called this morning."

"Ugh! Katrina. Does she have some sort of radar that tells her when you're happy so she can call and make your life miserable?"

"That's highly possible. After all, she is gifted," Krista said, smiling in spite of herself.

"Honestly," Gina sputtered. "I used to wish I hadn't been born an only child, but your sisters almost make me glad. How in the world anyone as warm and caring as you ever ended up in the same family as your three older sisters is beyond me."

"I think it's beyond them, too," Krista confessed. "At one point, they were sure that there must have been some mix-up at the hospital and that somewhere out there, their *real* sister was growing up just like them."

The morning light reflected off Gina's wild blond hair as she shook her head and rolled her blue eyes. "What did Katrina want this time?" she asked.

"She wanted to warn me against 'becoming romantically involved with *that* baseball player.'"

"How did Katrina know you were seeing Will?" Gina asked.

"I'm not seeing Will!"

"I think kissing him in the kitchen constitutes seeing him, Krista. Anyway, you were saying?"

Krista took another sip of coffee, then finally said, "I mentioned the fact that Will gave Tommy a baseball glove. After that, I didn't get a word in edgewise."

"Sometimes I wonder why you don't just hang up on her," Gina grumbled.

"She's right."

"Tell me you don't actually agree with Katrina about something."

"I know it's scary, but really, Gina. When it comes to love, I've always let my body rule my mind. I react to Will ten times faster than I've ever reacted to anyone else. One kiss, and I go up in smoke. I can't go sight-seeing with him today."

Krista saw her friend's eyes widen. After a long pause during which Gina lowered her eyebrows and took a deep breath, she finally said, "You didn't tell me he asked you to go sight-seeing. Why don't you tell me why you *can't* go."

"Because, if he kisses me again, I'm not sure I'd want him to stop," Krista whispered.

"Would that really be so bad?"

"What if he leaves me again?" Krista whispered.

"What if he doesn't?"

Krista was so caught up in Gina's question she barely noticed that the coffee she was sipping was getting cold. "What do you mean?" she asked, her voice seeming to come from far, far away.

"I mean," Gina began, "how do you know he's going to leave?"

"Baseball has always been his life."

"I know you swore you'd never follow another man, that you'd rely on yourself for your own happiness, but you said Will has changed. You said he didn't seem all that excited about the fact that his baseball buddies were in town. Maybe he's having a change of heart."

A change of heart.

Krista thought about the night Will had shown up on her doorstep with panic in his eyes. He'd sat in this very kitchen that night and told her that baseball had lost some of its magic. And last night, he really *hadn't* seemed very excited when he'd told her the guys were in town. Was he having second thoughts about returning to baseball?

She'd been trying to shore her heart against him since the moment she'd seen him again. Now, hope whispered through her mind and seeped past her barricades.

"How did he ask you?" Gina asked. "I mean, did he seem serious or intense?"

Krista chewed on her lower lip as she thought about Gina's question. "Actually, he was pretty nonchalant about the whole thing. He told me he'd call me today, after I'd had some time to think about it."

"If he was nonchalant, it doesn't sound to me as if he's going to push you into anything you don't want. Maybe it's a male ego thing. Maybe he wants to repay you for helping him learn to walk again. So let him fulfill his obligation. What's the worst that could happen?"

What's the worst thing that could happen? He could kiss her again. Or was that the best thing that could happen?

The slamming of the back door announced that Tommy was home. He was sauntering toward her, five or six strands of hair on top of his head bowing and swaying as always. He dropped the baseball glove on the counter and cast her a happy grin.

"I just caught forty-nine balls out of fifty. That's a ninety-eight percent average."

Krista smiled back at him and ruffled his soft hair, welcoming the diversion. "That's my boy," she bragged.

Tommy asked Gina about the triplets, who were home with their father. Krista watched the exchange between her son and her best friend, love and pride filling her chest.

Tommy really was her boy. Her child. From the moment he was born, she'd vowed to do her best to give him a good life. When he'd been able to name all the presidents when he was only two years old, her suspicions that he was brighter than the average toddler had been confirmed. That day she'd become more determined than ever to give him a normal childhood.

She knew what it was like to grow up feeling different, not because she was gifted, but because her sisters were and she wasn't. Her mother was gone now, but Krista couldn't help wondering if it would have been better for Katrina, Kimberly and Kendra if their mother had let them attend regular schools instead of those for child prodigies. Maybe they wouldn't have grown up to be so opinionated and critical of themselves and one another.

She wanted more for her son. She wanted him to have friends. So far, he had one. She wanted him to carve pumpkins and to believe in Santa Claus, to run and play, to make noise and get dirty. More than anything, she wanted to protect him from hurt and from harm, and at the same time make him strong and sure and proud. Good heavens, her thoughts were beginning to remind her of an advertisement for the Marines.

"Did Mommy tell you that Mrs. Santa Claus is working with her at the rehab center?"

Tommy's question broke into Krista's reverie.

"No, she didn't, Tommy," Gina replied.

"She's going to ask Mrs. Hall to take me there after school on Wednesday to meet her. Isn't that cool?"

Krista met Gina's smile. "That's cool, Tommy," her friend said sincerely.

"I tried to talk her into taking me to work with her so I wouldn't have to go to school at all, but she said no," Tommy said dejectedly.

Looking on, Krista wondered what it would take to make her son like school. If only the other boys would accept him.

"Mom? Can I play my new computer game now?" Tommy asked.

Krista nodded, and Tommy spun around, two coffee cups clattering in their saucers as sixty pounds of perpetual motion headed for the living room.

"*Mrs.* Santa Claus?" Gina asked.

Shrugging, Krista said, "I wanted him to believe in Christmas magic."

Dubiously eyeing her cup, Gina said, "I've never been able to figure out how a child so small can shake the entire house."

"He's all boy, all right," Krista agreed.

"Boys and girls are definitely different, aren't they?"

Krista nodded, glancing in the direction Tommy had just gone.

Gina slanted her a coy smile and said, "Men and women are, too. Aren't you glad?"

Krista made a face into her cold coffee. "You're lucky Tommy didn't ask you if *you* were having X-rated thoughts."

Grinning, Gina replied, "I probably would have told him to eat his popcorn, like you did."

Krista shook her head, a grudging smile pulling at her lips.

"So, what are you and Will going to see this afternoon?" Gina asked.

"What makes you think I'm going?"

"Because," Gina answered in a soft voice full of honest affection. "If you don't go, you'll never know what could have been. You'll never know if Will has changed, or if you could have trusted him with your heart."

Krista blinked the tears from her eyes. She'd been doing that a lot lately. She knew her emotions were operating on overload. She also knew that Gina was right. She was going to go sight-seeing with Will today. Maybe by the end of the afternoon, she'd know what he planned to do with the rest of his life. If he was going to leave Pennsylvania, she wanted to make sure he didn't take her heart with him when he left.

Six

―――――

The door was pulled open before Will could knock, giving him a hazy first impression of gold-colored jeans and a straw-colored shirt, of long dark hair waving freely around a heart-shaped face....

"Would you come inside for a minute?" Krista asked, turning so quickly that he didn't have time for more than a hurried nod.

He followed her inside, forcing himself to move slowly. She'd agreed to go out with him, and the last thing he wanted to do was break his leg tripping over his own two feet. She'd paced to the far side of the room, as jumpy as a cat on hot bricks. Will couldn't help wondering why.

He'd thought about her late into the night, and woke up in a drowsy tangle of sheets this morning so consumed by desire that he could barely move. Last night his invitation to go sight-seeing had come out of left field. Her acceptance this morning had come out of the blue.

Glancing around the living room at all the textures Krista loved, he tried to think of some way to put her at ease. "Where's Tommy?"

"He went down the street to show one of the boys in his class his new baseball glove," she replied. "I'm hoping that new ball glove will break the ice and they'll strike up a friendship. He'll be back in a few minutes, so we don't have much time to talk."

Will wasn't sure he liked the seriousness in her expression or in her voice. When her smile had lit up her eyes last night, he thought he'd seen stars. It had reminded him of her belief in his abilities to reach for the stars. Suddenly, it had seemed as if she was the star he was reaching for. That's when he'd blurted out his invitation to go sight-seeing. At the time, he'd been worried that he was moving too fast. He didn't want to rush her, but he wasn't used to taking things slowly.

"What do you want to talk about?" he asked.

"I think we need to set up a few more ground rules."

More ground rules. Great. He didn't want to set up ground rules. He wanted to stroll with her down to her bedroom and take up where his dreams had left off.

Gazing at her across the small room, he felt as if he were facing a pitcher who knew his swing by heart. That's when it dawned on him. Krista thought she knew exactly what he was going to do. She expected him to rush in and try to sweep her off her feet, straight onto her back.

For the first time since she'd opened the door, his thoughts cleared and the thread of a plan began to form in his mind. Of course she expected him to rush her. It's what the men in her life had always done. Hell, he knew she'd been hurt, terribly hurt. He wanted to tell her he wouldn't hurt her for the world.

"Mind if I sit down?" he asked.

She nodded, and he lowered the zipper on his lightweight jacket and slowly eased his frame into the soft cushions of her couch. Patting the cushion next to him, he said, "Don't you want to sit down, too?"

Will cast her what he hoped was his most endearing grin and almost hooted out loud when her brows went up and her chin went down. He'd surprised her. Ha! This was only the beginning.

She stepped around the coffee table and sat down. The sound her shirt made as it brushed along the back of the sofa reminded him of satin swishing to the floor. His pulse quickened and his gaze strayed to her shoulders, slowly moving lower.

The refrigerator hummed from the next room. Otherwise, the house was completely quiet. Deep inside him, his body began to throb and all thoughts except one slowly drained away. He wanted this woman. In every way, and in any way.

She cleared her throat and fidgeted with her collar. Will's heart thumped in his chest. His mind floundered. He'd had a plan. Why in blazes couldn't he remember what it was?

Slowly, his thoughts cleared. He'd wanted to put her at ease. He'd wanted to show her that he wasn't like Tommy's father or her boyfriend back in high school. He'd wanted to show her that *he* liked her for what was on the inside. Will doubted that his gaping stare was accomplishing any of those goals.

Swallowing hard, he forced himself to settle down. Still, when he spoke, his voice broke into a hoarse whisper. "About those ground rules."

"Well," she began. "First of all, I'd appreciate it if you wouldn't mention this to anybody at the rehab center."

Remembering when she'd told him about the gossip surrounding her relationship with Tommy's father, Will didn't think that was an unrealistic request. "That's fine with me," he answered. "I've been featured in the tabloids too many times not to appreciate a little privacy. What else?"

Krista swallowed. Will was staring at her mouth, and it was all she could do to keep from wetting her lips. Something about him was different today. It wasn't his hair. The brown strands were still streaked with honey blond and were still slightly askew in the front. It wasn't the glint in his sky blue eyes or the faint stubble on his chin, either. It was something else, something she couldn't put her finger on.

She'd thought about her conversation with Gina all morning. What if Will *had* had a change of heart? What if he really didn't want to go back to baseball? Had he really come over last night just to see her smile? Is that why he'd kissed her? On the other hand, what if all he felt was gratitude because she'd agreed to help him learn to walk again?

She placed her fingers to her forehead and closed her eyes. Questions. There were so many questions. And Krista wanted to find the answer to every one. The problem was, she couldn't think straight when Will was looking at her like that. More than anything, she couldn't think straight when he kissed her.

Opening her eyes again, she studied the room, the woven throw on the back of the chair, the flowered rug beneath her feet. It had taken her a long time to decorate this room, but it had taken her even longer to find the inner peace she felt here. It wasn't going to be easy to break her vow to swear off men. But then, Krista had never been accustomed to things that were easy.

"What else did you want to talk about, Krista?"

"We're going out today as friends who are getting to know each other again. I'd like us to end the day the same way. Therefore, I don't think it would be a very good idea for us to, well, to... kiss."

From the corner of her eye, she saw his head jerk around so fast that she was surprised he didn't get whiplash. "You don't think we should kiss?" he asked incredulously.

"I think it would be better if we didn't."

"Ever?"

Finally, she turned to him, secretly amused at his skepti-cal expression. "It would be less confusing," she stated.

Less confusing, Will thought to himself. It might be less confusing, but it would also be next to impossible.

His pulse was pounding like bongo drums, but a few things about Krista were starting to make sense. He was fi-nally beginning to understand why she'd sworn off men. She'd always been gorgeous, and time had only added to her beauty. Most men didn't have too much trouble showing a woman how they felt about her body. Krista needed him to show her how beautiful she was on the inside. It occurred to him that it was going to take more than mere words to break down all the barricades she'd erected around her heart. And she'd just given him the means with which to do it.

An unexpected excitement surged through him. Leaning closer, he slid his arm along the back of the sofa, letting his fingers toy with the wisps of hair feathering her ear. He looked directly into her eyes and quietly said, "Those are some ground rules."

He saw her gaze settle to his mouth, and fought against the impulse to lean closer and touch his lips to hers.

"Then it's okay with you?"

"I'll tell you what," he whispered, smoothing his finger-tip across her lower lip. "If that's what you want, I give you my word. I won't kiss you . . . unless you ask."

The back door slammed and a picture frame rattled across the room as Tommy came inside. "Mommy?"

"We're in here," she called.

Scooting to the edge of the sofa, she cast a quick glance at Will and asked, "Is that a promise?"

Keeping his voice calm, he nodded slowly. "I won't pre-tend that it's going to be easy, but yes, Krista. That's a promise." Holding up two fingers, he added, "Scout's honor."

For a moment Tommy's face was long, but the instant he saw Will, his entire expression brightened. He made a beeline for Will's side and looked up at him with huge brown eyes.

"How did Dustin like your new glove?" Krista asked.

"He wasn't home," Tommy answered. "I'll try again later." Turning his attention back to Will, he asked, "Were you a Boy Scout when you were little?"

Will pulled a baseball cap from his pocket and plunked it on Tommy's head. Grinning down at the boy, he shrugged and said, "Since I can't tell a lie, I have to say no, Tommy, I wasn't a Boy Scout."

"Neither am I. Cool."

Will turned his most beguiling grin to Krista and smiled as innocently as could be. Her eyes grew large as she stared wordlessly at him. The next thing he knew, she tipped her head up, laughter floating out of her. The warm, rich sound echoed through the house, echoing inside Will.

He'd never met anyone whose laughter heated his mind and body as fast as Krista's did. God, she was beautiful. So warm and sultry and feminine. His thoughts slowed as realization dawned. She was the most sensuous woman he'd ever known, and he'd just promised *not* to kiss her.

Another notion crept into his mind, bringing with it a much more pleasurable sensation. He'd promised not to kiss her...unless she asked him to.

Anticipation surged inside him, pushing through every vein until it settled into the very center of him. Before he was finished, she was going to ask him to kiss her. Boy, was she going to ask.

"Did you know that Philadelphia is the city of brotherly love?" Tommy asked from the back seat.

"I think I've heard that somewhere," Will said, glancing at Tommy in his rearview mirror.

The kid was a hoot, even if he did talk a mile a minute. He was endearing and cute. He might very well have been the brightest six-year-old Will had ever met, but that little boy was completely oblivious to the silent pulse of attraction spreading outward like radio waves each time Will looked into Krista's eyes.

He'd promised not to kiss her, but that hadn't kept him from glancing at her lips time and time again. It hadn't kept him from touching her, either. Somehow managing to keep his touch gentle, he'd smoothed a lock of hair from her cheek and brushed his fingertips down her arm. Each brief contact intensified his need, his desire.

They'd been driving on and off for the past hour. Exclaiming over the valleys dotted with rocks, weeds, shrubs and bushes in a dozen different shades of gold and yellow, they took turns pointing at the hills covered with trees of crimson, gold and amber. Will didn't care that the color had "peaked" more than a week ago, or that the clouds were so thick that they seemed to touch the ground in every direction. He was seeing Pennsylvania through Krista and Tommy's eyes, and he was enjoying every minute.

So far, they'd toured two of Bucks County's covered bridges and were heading south to see the South Perkasie Covered Bridge. He wouldn't have had to bother picking up a brochure along the way; Tommy was a fountain of information all by himself. He rattled off the names of all eleven covered bridges in Bucks County, slipping in tidbits of information about each and every one. The names of the covered bridges were fascinating in themselves, names like the Loux and the Cabin Run Covered Bridges, Mood's, Erwinna and the Pine Valley bridges, but witnessing them through a child's perspective was even better.

"Are we almost there?" Tommy asked.

Will took his eyes from the road long enough to look at Krista. *Were they almost there?* The sign they'd just passed had announced that the bridge was one mile away. Relatively speaking, they might have been almost there, but Will had a purpose, a plan, and it was going to extend a lot further than the next mile.

Krista waited to answer Tommy's question until her quickened pulse subsided. "We're getting closer," she said softly.

She cast a sidelong glance at Will. His eyes were on the road, but she didn't miss the tiny smile playing along his lips, those boyishly pouty sensuous lips. Her pulse quickened all over again.

The desire inside the car was as thick as the clouds in the sky. She'd told Will she wouldn't kiss him. She hadn't said it because she didn't want to, but because she couldn't think clearly when they kissed. *Not* kissing him wasn't helping to clear her thoughts. All *not kissing* him was doing was making her think about kissing him.

"Did you know that covered bridges used to be called *kissing bridges?*" Tommy asked.

"I like the sound of that," Will declared.

With a shake of her head, she dropped her face into both her hands. When she looked back up again, Tommy was giggling and Will was grinning. She gave up, and laughed right along with them.

Their laughter lightened the mood, but it didn't chase the anticipation away completely. Will parked the car, and the three of them meandered along the path toward the bridge. "Look at that, Mommy," Tommy said, pointing to a vintage sign of the era that was attached to the bridge.

Krista read the words on the sign out loud. "Five Dollars Fine For Any Person Riding Or Driving Over This Bridge Faster Than A Walk Or Smoking Segars On."

"You can imagine what a smoldering cigar could have done to an old wooden bridge," Will said quietly.

Krista could imagine, all right. A smoldering cigar could set the bridge on fire, much the way Will's deep voice was doing to her.

"Come on," Tommy said, pulling on her hand.

The bridge was fifteen feet wide and ninety-three feet long. The planks were old, the interior shaded. Strolling beneath the bridge's roof, Krista felt as if she'd stepped back into a simpler time. Safe inside the old structure, she was just a woman with a child, a woman who was enjoying the company of a very special man.

They walked the entire length of the wooden bridge, then slowly made their way back toward the car, Tommy keeping up a steady stream of conversation all the while. By the time they pulled away and headed east, his questions were growing shorter, and the spans of silence in between longer.

They drove through the back roads of Pennsylvania, she and Tommy laughing right along with Will as he regaled them with stories about friends named Joe, Arnie and Danny Boy. They talked about his family back in Nebraska, about the weather, the rehab center, and just about everything else under the sun.

"I can see why you love it here in Pennsylvania," he said, pointing to a particularly beautiful patch of scenery. "But how did you wind up in Coopersburg?"

"You probably won't believe this," Krista said, "but I'd have to say it was fate. I was working at the Fourth Street Rehab Center and Tommy and I were living in an apartment in Allentown. He's always been a beautiful child, but even as a tiny baby, he didn't want to close his eyes in case he missed something. To this day I swear he's his most charming after midnight."

She talked on, but Will's imagination couldn't get beyond the phrase *most charming after midnight*. It had an oddly provocative quality to it. Will would have liked nothing better than to show her how charming *he* could be after midnight.

Krista was still talking. Running his hand across his chin, he knew it required every ounce of willpower he possessed to tamp down his desire and concentrate on what she was saying.

"I've always said he was too inquisitive to be content. No matter what I tried, he fought against falling asleep. Except when he was riding in the car. Needless to say, I used to take him for drives every chance I had. I met Gina at a little diner in Coopersburg on one of those little nap excursions. We struck up a friendship instantly, and two years later, I'd saved enough money for a down payment on my house, and Tommy and I moved here.''

Will heard the affection in Krista's voice. He wondered if she was aware that there had also been weariness. She was raising a child single-handedly. He knew that wasn't such a rare occurrence nowadays, but that didn't detract from how difficult it must be. She had a son, a job, a mortgage and bills, and a heart bigger than all those things combined.

The atmosphere inside the car had grown quiet. Glancing into the back seat, he whispered, ''Look. I think riding in a car still has the same effect on Tommy.''

The child had fallen asleep. His baseball cap was crooked, his little head resting against the door. He looked so innocent that it sent an almost painful ache to Will's chest.

''Did you ever go to Tommy's father for financial help?'' he asked.

He sensed more than saw her shake her head.

''The courts would have forced him to pay child support,'' he said quietly.

''I thought about it. I even went to him once to talk about it. But he had something else on his mind, something else entirely.''

Will swore under his breath. The way she'd said ''something else entirely'' left little doubt that she was referring to sex. That jerk. No wonder she'd sworn off men.

The tires of his car churned over the loose gravel of a curving road much the way his thoughts churned through his mind. Catching her hand in his own, he finally said, ''Is that when you stopped smiling?''

Krista stared straight ahead and softly replied, ''I smile.''

''Sure you do,'' he answered.

He pulled off the road onto what could only be called a path. "Where are you going?" she asked.

"It looks as if this path winds to the top of the hill. I'll bet the view is beautiful from there."

They rode on in silence for the next few minutes, bumping over ruts and potholes the size of small copper mines. When they reached the top of the hill, Will pulled away from a stand of trees, threw the lever into park and turned the key. "Come on," he said quietly, reaching over the back seat for his crutches. "Let's have a look at that view."

They both closed their doors as quietly as possible so not to wake Tommy. Krista rounded the front of the car and stood next to Will, who was leaning heavily on his crutches. They'd walked across three covered bridges, not to mention all the ground they'd covered traipsing from parking lots and along the roads leading to and from the bridges. Now that he no longer wore his leg braces, he must have been exhausted.

"Are you beginning to feel the day in every muscle?" she asked quietly.

In answer, he used the muscles in his arms and shoulders to position himself up on the hood of his car. With his feet dangling over the side, he spread his arms wide and said, "I'm okay, but *feel* that view."

Krista leaned her hip against the car, looking all around her. The clouds were so low that she could practically reach up and touch them, the colors below too beautiful for words. The clouds gave everything a muted-watercolor quality, one color blending into another. Overhead, geese honked on their way by. She brought her hand to the back of her neck, gently kneading the knot that had formed there from riding.

Will's large hand covered her own as he said, "You've been massaging my muscles for weeks. Come here and let me return the favor."

Before she knew it, she was standing between his knees, her back to him. He fitted his hands to her shoulders, gently kneading, slowly moving his fingers and palms up to her neck and back again. She let her head fall forward and her eyelids drop down, oblivious to everything except the feel of Will's hands stroking over her flesh, his fingers working the stress from tendons and muscles.

She wasn't sure how long they stood like that. After a time she became aware that a light mist had begun to sift down from the clouds, reminding Krista that it was time to go. Before they left, there was one thing she wanted to know. "Is that why you asked me to come along today? Because you wanted to return a favor?"

His fingers stilled and the pressure in his grip changed. He turned her around to face him. A thin sheen of moisture clung to his skin and the breeze ruffled his hair, momentarily blowing hers into her eyes. He smoothed the strands away with both hands, carefully tucking her hair behind her ears.

"I asked you to spend the day with me because I want to be with you. Gratitude has nothing to do with it. Even though I've never been a Boy Scout, I hope you believe me."

His wry humor touched her almost as much as his explanation. She believed him, and it had nothing to do with whether he'd ever been a Boy Scout. Dreaminess settled over her as he traced the outline of her face with the pad of one finger. As he leaned closer, his breath touched her lips, and her eyelashes fluttered down, the dreaminess turning to warmth.

He's going to kiss me. The mist surrounded her in softness as she waited for the touch of his lips.

"Ah, Krista," he said softly, not more than a breath away from her own mouth. "How I wish I hadn't made that promise."

His words finally filtered through her entrancement. She opened her eyes, watching as he lifted his face. His eyes were half closed, his pupils trained on her mouth. He raised his face a few more inches, and quietly said, "But a promise is a promise. I'm not going to kiss you. Not unless you ask."

His arms were straight down, both hands flattened along the hood of the car. Cold filtered through Krista's jeans where her legs were pressed tight to the car's side. Will's knees were bent, his thighs straddling her waist. She wasn't sure how her hands had come to rest along his upper legs, but one glance left little doubt what her touch had done to him.

She looked into his eyes for a long moment, the desire she saw there mirroring her own. *I'm not going to kiss you. Not unless you ask.* She'd told Gina that she was going out with Will today to see if he'd changed. She hadn't gotten around to asking about his plans for the future, but she knew he'd changed. He'd made a promise, and he'd kept it.

She took a backward step, her hands falling away from his thighs. Walking around the front of the car, she was afraid to place too much optimism in one tiny promise. Hope somehow found its way inside her just the same. If he had been looking, he'd have seen her smile.

A gust of wind swirled through Will's open jacket and whipped Krista's hair into her eyes. He saw her reach up with both hands to twist the strands securely at her nape and tuck them into the collar of her tweed jacket. She seemed oblivious to his stare, but the expression on her face was one of joy.

His blood thundered through his veins. He'd kept his promise to her, but it hadn't been easy. His reward had been her smile. Although nothing had been said, everything had changed. Crutches or not, it was all he could do not to strut.

He stowed his crutches in the back seat and started the car, hoping he wasn't grinning like an idiot. He didn't need to be hit over the head with a ton of bricks to know that this was no longer simply a case of a man wanting a woman. He was still hard-pressed to put a name to the feeling, but one of these days he would.

"It looks like the rain is calling an end to our sight-seeing," Krista said after the car began its bumpy descent of the hill.

Taking his eyes from the curving path, he said, "I've enjoyed every minute of it. Thanks for showing me your Pennsylvania."

Will was so busy watching her he didn't see the rut in the road until it was too late. The left front tire fell in, then bounced out again. "Sorry about that," he said when the rear tire followed the same path.

"Wow, what was that?" Tommy asked, suddenly awake in the back seat.

"That was what happens when a man's mind is on something other than his driving," Will answered.

"Cool!" Tommy exclaimed. "Could you do it again?"

"I don't think that would be a very good idea," Krista answered before Will could say what he was thinking.

"Spoilsport," Will mouthed.

The windshield wipers swished back and forth, and Krista was pretty sure her heartbeat was keeping time. So many feelings were rising inside her that it was difficult to concentrate on only one. There was tenderness and admiration and yearning and others she couldn't even name.

Tommy did most of the talking on the drive back to Coopersburg. Krista welcomed the reprieve. It allowed her to sit back and listen. And think.

She'd agreed to go sight-seeing with Will today because she'd wanted to get to know him again. When he'd promised not to kiss her, she'd thought the matter was settled. How was she supposed to know that *she'd* forget all about her own stipulation twice in one afternoon? But Will hadn't forgotten. Why did that fact make her feel like singing?

The rain had let up, and far into the east it looked as if the clouds were starting to break apart. The car pulled into her driveway and, suddenly, it seemed as if the afternoon was over too soon.

"Can I unlock the back door, Mommy?" Tommy asked.

Krista handed him the key and watched as he pushed out of the car and ran toward the side door. "He's in such a hurry to grow up," she said to Will.

"Aren't all kids?" he asked.

"I guess you're right, but you really made his day today, and I just want to say thanks," she said, glancing out the side window where she could see Tommy painstakingly fitting the key into the lock. "It looks as if it's stopped raining for good. I promised Tommy I'd order pizza for supper. I'm sure he'd love it if you'd stay."

She turned around slowly and found that Will had been watching Tommy, too. In the process, he'd leaned closer. As she settled back into her seat, her shoulder brushed his, and his gaze slowly met hers. For a moment, she studied him intently. His lips looked moist, and his eyes were darker than she'd ever seen them.

"What do you say?" she asked quietly. "Would you like to come inside?"

She wasn't sure who leaned closer, she or he, but as if by magic, his lips were only inches from hers. "I'd better not," he whispered.

"Why?" she asked, her voice trailing away dreamily.

"Because if I come inside, I'm going to have an awfully hard time keeping my promise."

Despite the softly spoken words, she saw a certain tenseness in his face, as if he was fighting a battle with his restraint and barely coming out ahead. It only intensified her growing feelings. She tipped her head slightly and said, "Then I guess this is goodbye."

"Krista?"

With her hand on the door handle, she turned around, waiting for his next words.

"I'll see you on Monday at the rehab center. Don't forget, mum's the word. In the meantime, if you want to change your latest ground rule, let me know."

She somehow managed to close the door and take a few steps back. Tommy waved exuberantly when Will honked the horn at the end of the driveway. Coming out of her befuddled state, Krista waved, too, then strode to the door where Tommy was waiting.

"Can I dial the telephone?" her son asked.

"The telephone?"

"Yeah," he answered, letting the screen door bang shut behind him. "You know, to order our pizza for supper. Mommy? Why are you smiling?"

"Don't I usually smile?" she asked.

"You smile at me, but this looks different. This looks more like the way they smile on soap operas on television. Can I order the pizza myself? Can I?"

Soap operas on television?

"Yes, honey," she answered. "I'll help you. But first..." she said, striding to the counter. "First I'm going to start a pot of coffee."

Seven

Calling goodbye to Heather and Brody, Krista hurried from the employee lounge. The entire floor was alive with activity this afternoon, patients and therapists alike making their way to and from exercise and therapy sessions. Mrs. A was a few steps ahead, and at the other end of the hall, Krista spotted Will.

Catching up with her white-haired friend, Krista asked, "Is that another blooming violet from your husband?"

Mrs. A looked up from the green tissue paper she was carefully removing from another plant. Nodding, she said, "Some men know the way to a woman's heart, don't they?"

Krista's gaze flickered over the other patients on the floor, automatically settling on the man who had promised not to kiss her. Some men definitely had a way with a woman's heart. Will Sutherland was one of them. He'd been his usual self during his therapy sessions this past week and a half, pushing himself to his limits and beyond, stubbornly refusing to listen to her one minute then casting her his most beguiling grin the next. She'd introduced him to his walker on Tuesday. Although he'd scoffed, he'd grasped the handles and proceeded to make his way all the way down the hall.

He'd shown up at her door that same night with all the fixings for a November picnic. He still hadn't kissed her, but she'd caught him looking at her mouth time and time again. She'd lost track of how many times he'd managed to slip the word *kiss* into the conversation. What was a woman supposed to do with a man like that?

Gina thought she should kiss him and get it over with. But Krista wasn't ready to do that. For the first time in her life, a man was waiting for *her* to make the first move. She was amazed at the sense of excitement that gave her.

The sound of crinkling paper drew her from her musings. Mrs. A held the beautiful plant up for Krista to see.

"Are you thinking about going back home?" Krista asked.

"I've always planned to go back home," the woman said. "Even though the boys are all grown and are proving to be very adept at handling the business, I couldn't bear to be away from them forever. But I had to leave for a little while. Why, even Nicholas was beginning to call me Mrs. A. But he's starting to come around to my way of thinking just as I hoped he would."

Krista stepped aside as a patient ambled by, and Mrs. A continued. "It's a good thing I didn't listen to my sisters all those years ago when they told me Nicholas was no good for me. Not that he hasn't been a mite stubborn at times, mind you. But he's also the most infinitely caring man I've ever known."

"Your sisters didn't approve of him?" Krista asked, turning her head slightly to look at her friend.

"Ach, my sisters and I are as different as night and day. Maybe it would have helped if our parents would have given me a winter name like theirs. But I'm glad they didn't," Mrs. A answered, a girlish smile spreading across her ageless face. "Nicholas loves my name. That's why it hurt so much when he quit calling me by it."

"What *is* your first name?" Krista asked, searching her mind and discovering that she always referred to her as Mrs. A, too.

"It's Violet, dear."

Krista felt a warm glow flow through her. "That's a beautiful name. Don't your sisters see how well it suits you?"

The older woman beamed from the compliment, saying, "Belle and Holly chose very traditional roles in life. Belle teaches music to the el—er, to the employees, and let's just say that Holly is into decorating. Neither of them ever married, and although they'd do anything for me, they're just a *trifle* opinionated. Nicholas loves to rattle them. My, yes, he gets a kick out of doing that."

Krista said, "My parents gave my sisters and I names that begin with the letter *K*, but we're still as different as night and day. They've never approved of anything I've ever done."

"Ach. You're one of the best therapists I know and you're doing a wonderful job of raising Tommy. . . ."

Up ahead, Will had reached the end of the hall and turned around. Krista knew the instant he noticed her, because his eyes filled with a warm expression and his lips lifted in that cocksure way of his that was impossible to ignore. Although there were several people on the floor, everything else receded to another plane.

"Why that little boy is delightful," Mrs. A prattled on. "You should be proud."

Without looking away from Will, Krista said, "I am proud of Tommy, Mrs. A, I mean, Violet. I don't know what you said to him last week, but he's been singing 'Jingle Bells' ever since."

"Why, I simply told him the truth...that I really am Mrs. Santa Claus."

As if in slow motion, Krista dragged her gaze from Will, who was now only a few steps away, and eyed her friend. *Mrs. Santa Claus?*

Violet winked at her, and Will said hello. Since nobody at the rehab center knew they were seeing each other, all Krista could do was return his greeting and walk on toward the room at the end of the corridor where her next patient was waiting.

Will grasped his walker with both hands. Turning his head, he watched Krista go. This walker was the damnedest contraption he'd ever seen, but it worked. Hot damn, but he felt good.

He'd tried to tell Krista she was responsible for his success. With raised eyebrows and wide brown eyes, she'd said, "Are you kidding? You've run away with your entire therapy program. Besides, I always knew you could do it."

Will could have told her she was wrong, that *she* had everything to do with the fact that he was learning to walk again, but he didn't think she was ready for his reasoning. Sure, he was stubborn. His coaches had told him that all his life. But his stubbornness had very little to do with the giant step he'd made in his recovery these past several weeks. It might have been sheer bullheadedness that had gotten him out of his wheelchair, but it was the unspent desire pushing through him that had shoved his adrenaline into high gear and got him walking again.

No, Krista definitely wasn't ready to hear that. Evidently, she wasn't ready to kiss him, either. *He,* on the other hand, was so ready that he could barely see straight.

It had been a week and a half since he'd told her he wouldn't kiss her. And he hadn't. But he'd touched her hand, her shoulder, her cheek. Each time he did, she looked at him intently, her eyelashes lowered and her lips parted. Those fleeting touches were like sparks falling on kindling.

One of these days a tiny ember was going to ignite into a glowing fire.

Will didn't know how much longer he could wait. He'd never taken so many cold showers in his life, and he was quite sure he was wearing a path in the gray carpet in his apartment. He wanted her with a force that surprised even him. Seeing her through the double doors up ahead, he knew he didn't want to rush her. But if she didn't make the first move soon, he was going to come apart at the seams.

"Just be careful you don't hurt her."

Will turned so quickly he almost lost his balance. Mrs. A reached a steadying hand toward him while he searched anxiously for the meaning behind her words. Krista didn't want the people at work to know about them. He'd tried not to let his feelings show, at least not here. She was gaining confidence in his word, but he was afraid rumors flying around the rehab center would send her belief in him straight back to zero.

"Don't worry," Mrs. A said with a sprightly wink. "Nobody else suspects a thing. The only reason I know is because I see things other people don't."

Staring into Mrs. A's eyes, Will knew she wasn't going to tell anybody what she suspected.

The older lady winked at him again and said, "It looks as if Tommy's going to get another of his Christmas wishes. My, how wonderful. And the timing couldn't be more perfect. This is marvelous. You remind me so much of my Nicholas when he was your age. He was a charmer, too. My, yes, he was. He used to come a-courting every Saturday night, a handsome smile on his face and a bouquet of violets in his hand. And violets weren't easy to come by in all that snow."

"Snow?" Will asked in confusion. What in the world was Mrs. A talking about?

"Never mind, dear," she insisted. "Just remember this. Krista couldn't help liking you, but it's the little things that win a woman's heart."

Mrs. A's voice contained a melodious quality, working over him like a song, the words replaying through his mind over and over again. *It's the little things that win a woman's heart.*

She'd said her husband had come a-courting with a bouquet of violets in his hand. Krista was no shrinking violet. She was more like a bright yellow daffodil, bravely poking its head up through the snow. Like that daffodil, there was a place deep inside her that was vulnerable and so darned fragile it took his breath away.

Mrs. A patted his arm before hurrying away to perform some task. Concentrating on putting one foot in front of the other, Will watched her go. What she'd said about courting and violets gave him an idea. He glanced back at Krista, his idea taking form. By the time he pushed through the outer doors a short time later, he felt like a school kid ten seconds before the final bell. The trek out to his car had never seemed shorter. Although the November wind had a chilly sting to it, he was far from cold.

"Will," Krista said, opening the front door wide. "I didn't expect to see you tonight."

His blue eyes darkened over a masculinely sensuous smile as he took a step closer. "I couldn't stay away."

There was something different about him tonight, an inner excitement, a deeper sensuality. The message in his eyes was so intense that Krista couldn't look away.

"I brought you something."

For the first time, she took her eyes from his, glancing at the package in his hand. "What is it?" she asked.

"Open it and see."

She took a moment to close the door behind him before saying, "You brought me flowers?"

"Not just any flowers. These have always reminded me of you."

She lifted the bright yellow paper from the plant, a soft gasp escaping her lips. Six daffodils bloomed in profusion in a short clay pot. "Oh, Will, they're beautiful."

"That's one of the reasons they remind me of you."

She'd changed into jeans and a cotton shirt once she got home from work. Wisps of hair had slipped from her french braid when she'd played catch with Tommy half an hour ago. She knew how she looked, but she was beginning to realize that faded jeans and windblown hair weren't what Will saw when he looked at her. He saw something she was only now beginning to understand.

"Daffodils really remind you of me?"

She'd always loved daffodils. They were daintily regal and full of the promise of spring. Was that really the way Will saw her?

That thought sent tenderness and sensuality and desire coursing through her. She'd only been with three men in her entire life. Her first time had been with her boyfriend in high school. She'd loved him the way a seventeen-year-old loves an eighteen-year-old, wholeheartedly, immaturely. Those early experiences with sex had been less than ideal. There had been a lot of fumbling and a lot of groping and a lot of heavy breathing. It wasn't until she met Will during her third year in college that she awakened to her true sensuality. She'd flown into Steven's arms on the rebound from Will, and although their lovemaking had been intense, it had lacked the intimacy she'd felt with Will.

Her sensuality had lain dormant for almost seven years. Why should the sight of six bright daffodils make her feel like Sleeping Beauty, waking up from a long, long sleep, warm and wanting in both mind and body?

It was because of Will.

She looked from the pot in her hand to the waistband on his low-slung jeans. He was wearing a washed-out Titans

T-shirt that had seen better days. As usual, his hands rested on the bars of his crutches, but now he was barely leaning on them for support.

Her gaze finally made it up to his chin, darkened with stubble as always, past his nose, to his eyes. He wasn't even trying to hide the fact that he was watching her. His openness fueled her feelings, the desire in his eyes drawing her near.

He didn't move, except to lower his chin. It was all the invitation Krista needed. Balancing the pot in one hand, she placed her other palm on Will's chest, lifting her face toward his. She kept her eyes half open, watching him with breath bated, waiting. *Kiss me,* she whispered in her mind.

"Uh, uh, uh," he chided so deeply and huskily that she barely heard. *Not until you ask* was written all over his face.

The kitchen door slammed and a light fixture rattled overhead. Tommy was back. At last, reluctantly, she stepped away. Waiting for her quickened pulse to subside, she wondered if Sleeping Beauty had ever asked her prince for a kiss.

"Oh, hi, Will," Tommy said forlornly. "Did you come to take us sight-seeing again?"

Will took a deep breath and tried to get his hormones under control. That near kiss had been a near miss. It had been all he could do to remind Krista of his promise. If Tommy hadn't slammed that door when he did, Will was pretty sure he would have said to hell with half-baked schemes and out-and-out promises and kissed her senseless.

"Hi, kiddo," Krista said. "What's wrong? Wasn't Dustin home?"

"He was home. Remember when you told me that Pennsylvania means Penn's Woods and was named for a Quaker who established a colony here so his fellow Quakers and other people who were different would fit in?"

Will watched the exchange between mother and son. That last question had been a mouthful, even for Tommy. For the life of him, Will didn't know what it had to do with the boy's sad expression.

"It didn't work," Tommy said gravely.

"What didn't work, honey?" Krista asked.

"Establishing a place where everyone would fit in. *I* don't fit in."

"Of course you do," she insisted. "You're a great kid."

"You're just saying that because you're my mother. Dustin Jamison says I'm a baby."

"Who cares what Dustin Jamison says?" Will interrupted.

"I care," Tommy answered truthfully. "He's the most popular boy in my class. I took my new ball glove over there tonight, but he didn't believe I got it from you."

Will felt his blood do a slow boil. Who did that other kid think he was, calling Tommy a baby and a liar? Why, he had half a mind to go over there right now and give that brat a piece of his mind.

Before Will could say a word, Tommy's voice quavered forlornly. "I was going to take my mitt and new baseball cap to school for show-and-tell tomorrow. Now I'm not going to."

Will choked down a string of cuss words. For a moment, the impulse to gather Tommy close and take him far, far away from hurt rendered him speechless.

"You should take the glove and hat in, anyway," Krista said softly. "So what if one boy doesn't believe you?"

Will looked from Krista to Tommy, an idea rushing into his mind like a pop-up fly to right field. "I have a better idea," he said quietly. "Tommy? How would you like to take Billy the Kid to show-and-tell?"

Tommy's eyes rounded. "Would you really do that?"

"I sure would. I hardly ever scratch and spit anymore, but with a little practice, I should be able to perfect them both. What do you say?"

"Cool!"

Will winked at Tommy's exuberance. With that, sixty pounds of wiry arms and legs attached to a skinny body and a dark-capped head came right at him. Will managed to stand his ground, the fingers on his right hand slowly spreading wide across the child's narrow back.

Suddenly, Will knew how the real Titans must have felt, barrel chested, strong and sure. That's how Tommy made him feel—like a giant who could hold the world in one hand.

Meeting Krista's gaze across the small room, he was reminded of how close he'd come to kissing her a few minutes ago. Tommy had interrupted because he'd needed them. There was need in Krista's eyes, too, and an answering one deep in the center of him. Soon, he said to himself. Soon, they'd all have what they needed.

Will made his way into Coopersburg Elementary School and headed for the office just as Krista had instructed. He was feeling incredibly lofty today, and it had nothing to do with the sunny November weather. When he'd pulled onto the highway and headed back toward Allentown last night anticipation had practically gripped his entire body. A day later, desire was still unfurling deep inside him.

The halls were lined with children's artwork, but it was the sound of high-pitched voices reciting multiplication tables that really took Will back to his own childhood. Man, he and Cort sure had given their teachers a run for their money.

A short, red-haired woman looked up when he entered the office. "Hi," Will said. "I'm..."

"You're Billy the Kid. I'd recognize you any day. Come in. I'm Alberta Mackelroy, principal of this school. I'll bet you didn't know that I'm one of your biggest fans, did you?"

Will found himself shaking his head as the diminutive woman who bore a striking resemblance to the woman who'd played the principal in *Kindergarten Cop* ran away with the conversation. She talked about Tommy's IQ and this year's enrollment while she filled out his name tag. Strangely, Will felt as if he were nine years old.

Before he knew it, he'd given the older woman his autograph and had promised her free tickets to next season's opening game. After making a grand production out of walking with him to the second-grade classroom, Mrs. Mackelroy strode inside. In a voice much larger than she was, she said, "Boys and girls, Tommy Wilson has a special surprise for you today. Tommy, would you come up front and introduce the friend you invited for show-and-tell?"

Will picked the boy out of the group, noticing the way he glanced shyly around the room. Catching his attention, Will winked and gestured for him to come on up. Tommy smiled at him, and once again Will felt seven feet tall. Damn, but this was heady.

The child opened his desk and removed the baseball glove and cap then strode up to the front of the class. He slid his small hand into his pocket and looked up at Will with eyes almost exactly the color of Krista's. Will winked again and squeezed the boy's shoulder for courage.

"Everybody," Tommy began, "I'd like you to meet Will Sutherland, also known as Billy the Kid. He plays baseball for the New York Titans, and he's the father I asked for for Christmas."

Uh, da, ubbada, da. Will couldn't form a coherent thought, let alone a coherent reply.

Some of the children sat in stony silence, others began to laugh. Will didn't know which was worse. He cast a slack-jawed look at Mrs. Mackelroy, and found her expression pretty much mirroring his own. Stephanie, Tommy's little friend, was sitting in the front row. Will couldn't tell if her mouth was open because it was hidden behind her hand.

Poor Tommy. Rooted to the spot as if frozen, he was the most horrified of all. Mrs. Hansen, the second-grade teacher, saved the day by calling for silence. "Children," she said. "Mr. Sutherland is a professional baseball player. Would any of you like to ask him a question?"

Twenty-four hands shot into the air.

"Let's start with the first row," Mrs. Hansen said. "Wes, what would you like to say?"

"Are you really Tommy's new father?"

Will should have been used to dodging weighted questions from inquisitive interviewers by now. Casting the look he'd perfected years ago all around the room, he said, "You know what a kidder Tommy is. He just said that to see if you were paying attention. But I'll tell you this. I'd be mighty proud if I really was his father."

He winked down at Tommy again. This time the boy returned a grin that was beguiling in its own right. Will settled himself onto a stool provided by the teacher and balanced his crutches on one knee.

A little boy with red hair went next. "Do you earn more than a million dollars playing baseball?"

Will glanced at the teacher, who shrugged helplessly. "Let's just say I do all right," he answered with a laugh.

One child asked him how old he was, and another asked if he'd ever played ball with Babe Ruth. A little girl with glasses and pigtails wanted to know about his accident, and the one after her asked, "Are you going to be able to walk again?"

Before Will could say a word, Tommy piped up and said, "Of course he is. My mom said he's already made incredible progress."

Will chuckled at Tommy's tone, but he had to admit that did sound like Krista. He ruffled the boy's hair and plucked the baseball cap from his hand, plopping it on Tommy's upturned head.

"Then you're going to play baseball next year?" A boy named Brett asked shyly.

Suddenly, all eyes turned to Will. Leave it to a little kid to ask a question the rest of America hadn't had the nerve to voice out loud. Eyeing all the children's eager expressions, Will didn't know what to say. He'd been dodging that question in his own mind for months. Baseball had been a magical dream for as long as he could remember. Somehow, somewhere along the way, it had lost its magic. The loss was acute, like a physical ache in his chest.

"That's a good question," he finally said. "To tell you the truth, I'm not sure what I'm going to do, but I doubt that I'll go back to professional ball."

Tommy looked up at him with wonder-filled eyes. The area surrounding Will's heart turned to mush, and the ache from the thought of leaving baseball lessened. There was hero worship deep inside the boy's eyes, but there was love, too. Suddenly, Will realized that there were other things in life besides baseball. And although change hurt, it also healed.

The remaining questions ranged from serious to silly. Will answered every one to the best of his ability. The kids all clapped when he was finished, and Tommy, the little urchin with the high IQ and the unfailing belief in Christmas wishes, gave him a high five.

Twenty-four high-pitched voices called goodbye as he made his way out of the classroom. Will took an autographed ball from his coat pocket and tossed it to Mrs. Mackelroy on his way by, chuckling out loud as her voice reached his ears. "Miss Stevens, I just caught a baseball thrown by Billy the Kid."

Stopping in his tracks, he retraced his steps to the open office door. Both women inside looked up as he said, "I just wanted to say thanks for allowing me to come today. But there's something you should know. Billy the Kid isn't a kid anymore."

The secretary didn't look as if she understood what he meant, but Mrs. Mackelroy nodded and smiled.

Swinging on out to the parking lot, Will recalled the wonder in Tommy's eyes when Will had told the class he'd be proud to be his father. Tired yet exhilarated, he let go of his dream of playing baseball and concentrated on another dream, one that included Krista. One that was just a kiss away.

Krista sat on the bed as Tommy kneeled and said his prayers. Evidently, her little boy had had a very good day, because his list of people to bless included every child in his class and a few she'd never heard of. Each time she was sure he was through, he thought of someone else to be thankful for. Normally, Krista wouldn't have minded, but tonight Will was waiting for her in the living room little more than a few dozen steps away.

"Amen," Tommy finally said, scampering onto the bed and underneath the covers.

Amen, Krista said to herself.

"Sleep tight, honey," she said, reaching for the light. "I sure do love you."

"Do you love Will, Mommy?"

Her hand stilled in midair. "Love him?" she asked softly.

"Yeah. Because it would sure help if you loved him. Stephanie said her mom fell in love with her new dad and now they're a family."

Smoothing her son's fine hair off his forehead, she said, "I know you like Will a lot, honey. But he and I haven't even mentioned love. He came here to learn how to walk again. We don't even know if he's going to go back to baseball."

"He isn't going back to baseball."

"What makes you think that?" she asked, becoming more worried about her son's feelings by the second.

"Because he told the whole class during show-and-tell today."

Leave it to Will to tell Tommy's second-grade class before he told her. Still, the knowledge was fast turning to hope.

"Will you at least try to love him?" Tommy asked, doing everything in his power to fight back a huge yawn.

Try? It wouldn't take much trying. "Close your eyes, sleepyhead," she whispered.

"I'm not tired," he said, finally losing the battle and yawning loudly.

"Then just rest your eyes for a minute," she returned, using a ploy that had worked countless times in the past.

"All right," he said sleepily, turning over onto his side. "Night, Mommy."

"Night, kiddo," she said, switching off the lamp and tiptoeing from the room.

Out in the living room, Will could hear the murmuring of soft voices from down the hall. Otherwise, the house was quiet. Tommy had pulled him aside when he'd first arrived, asking him not to mention anything to Krista about wanting a father for Christmas. "If everybody knows about my Christmas wish, it'll never come true," the boy had whispered.

Will had promised, and he didn't think he'd ever forget the way that little kid had smiled. It was the kind of smile filled with peaceful wonder. Instead of making him feel like a giant, this time it had made him weak in the knees. He was beginning to *feel* like a father to Tommy. It was the most humbling experience he'd ever had.

A door creaked ever so slightly as it was pulled closed. Turning, Will watched as Krista walked into the room. "It sounds as if Tommy's show-and-tell was a success," she whispered.

Will nodded. She walked farther into the room, folding her arms at her ribs in a way he'd come to recognize. "You've really decided not to go back to baseball?" she asked in a voice barely more than a whisper.

Will reacted to her honesty and straightforwardness the way he always did. With admiration and unfurling desire. Krista had never been one to beat around the bush. Wasn't that one of the reasons he'd come to her in the first place?

Spreading his arms wide over the back of the sofa, he crossed his ankles, still marveling that his muscles responded to his brain's command.

He waited to explain until she sat on the cushion next to him. "I told my manager this afternoon. He doesn't want me to rush into anything, but I've been on the verge of making this decision for months."

He wasn't sure what was going on behind her eyes. She stared at him for long seconds, as if reading every nuance in his expression. "Oh, Will," she said on a husky whisper. "I'm so sorry. I know how much you've always loved the game."

Why wasn't he surprised that she'd seen the faint thread of sadness in his eyes, sadness over leaving something he'd once loved with a passion? "I've never wanted your sympathy, Krista," he said, his voice shakier than he would have liked. Leaning closer, he asked, "Is there anything you want from me?"

For weeks Krista had felt as if her dormant sexuality was rousing from a deep sleep. Now it came to life inside her, graceful and pliant and infused with heat. She wet her lips, watching as Will's eyelids dropped partway. Sitting there so close to him, she thought about how difficult these past four months had been for him. His accident had been more than a curve in the road; it had been a crossroad. She knew he could have gone back to baseball. After all, he could do anything he put his mind to.

Will Sutherland was a special man.

"There is one thing you could do for me," she said in a broken whisper.

He moved a little closer. Waiting.

"Do you remember when we talked about all the French things I love?" she asked.

His gaze slid down to her mouth.

"I'd like to try one of them with you," she said.

His lips parted on a sudden intake of breath. "Are you asking?" he said in a voice that broke with huskiness.

Deliberately misinterpreting his question, she said, "For a date? Yes. I thought we could begin with that French restaurant you promised me."

"And after that?" he whispered.

Krista looked up at him, the desire in his eyes sending messages of wants and needs to the very center of her. "It's been a long time since I've been completely spontaneous, Will. Let's see where dinner takes us."

His eyes closed. He sat back slowly and ran his palm across his chin. "Tomorrow night?" he asked.

"Tomorrow night."

He stood and turned to look directly at her. Within seconds, his lips lifted into the cocky grin that was the essence of the man himself. "Tomorrow night, Krista. I can hardly wait to see what you have in store for us."

Eight

Will pulled into Krista's driveway the following day and reached for his new cane. He'd just advanced to using it this afternoon. Although he was thrilled to be able to walk without a walker or crutches, his thoughts had been hazy all day. His mind drifted over these past several weeks, continuously coming back to the scene playing out in his imagination, a scene in which he and Krista walked hand in hand to her bedroom.

All the cold showers in the world wouldn't put the fire out inside him tonight. One minute he wished dinner was over so he and Krista could make love, and the next he wanted to take the night so slow that it would never end.

She opened the door slowly, and he was left with more than hazy impressions. She was wearing an elegant dark purple dress with long sleeves and a V-neckline. The dress was formfitting but not tight. It stopped maybe six inches above slender ankles encased in sheer black nylons and feet arched in high-heeled black shoes.

The porch light glinted off her coffee-colored hair styled loosely on top of her head. She turned her head, one dangling earring catching a beam of yellow light, Krista's beauty catching him between the eyes.

"You have to know you're beautiful."

Raising her eyes to his, she smiled a woman's smile and said, "I like the way you say it."

He'd thought about her late into last night, and woke up in the drowsy warmth of his bed in the throes of a passion so strong that even breathing required careful thought. If she didn't ask him to kiss her tonight, he might just go out of his mind.

He followed her inside, where he patted the collar of his crisp white shirt. Smoothing his hand down his flowered tie, he glanced around the living room behind her at all the textures she loved. She'd decorated the room by touch. As far as he was concerned, she could touch him all night long.

He studied her face unhurriedly, feature by feature. She'd never worn much makeup for work, at least not that he could see, but there was a subtle difference in her appearance tonight. What a woman did with all those bottles and tubes had always been a mystery to Will. All he knew was that tonight Krista's eyelashes were darker and thicker than ever. Her skin looked as flawless and smooth as fine satin, her eyes large and luminous.

Her long earrings reflected the glow of lamplight, wisps of coffee-colored tresses touching her ears and the collar of her dress. "What do you call that hairstyle?" he asked on a whisper.

Smoothing a lock of hair off her forehead, she said, "It's a variation of a French twist."

Another French creation he'd forever associate with Krista.

"Is something wrong?" she asked.

Her lips had moved slowly over her words, drawing his gaze to her mouth. She was wearing lipstick the color of dark wine that made her lips look full and moist. He'd have loved nothing better than to kiss her until it was completely off.

"Wrong?" he finally asked, slowly coming out of his musings. Desire thrummed through his body, deepening his thoughts and his voice. "Nothing's wrong. In fact, everything is incredibly right."

He waited while she checked her purse and took a long coat from the living room closet. Holding the coat for her, he asked, "Where's Tommy?"

"He's spending the night at Stephanie's."

"The whole night?" He could tell by the look she cast him over her shoulder that she knew his imagination was running wild. She stepped around the coffee table, the light scent of her perfume reaching his nostrils a moment before the faint sound of satin swishing against satin reached his ears. His pulse quickened and his gaze strayed to her legs as her coat settled into place.

Deep inside him, his body began to throb as all thoughts except one slowly drained from his mind. She glanced up at him and caught him staring. Their eyes locked, and his heart thumped in his chest. Keeping his voice calm, he asked, "Are you ready?"

When she nodded, it was all he could do to keep from slipping her coat off her shoulders and beginning the evening the way he wanted it to end. One step at a time, he whispered under his breath. One step at a time.

Krista was aware of the attraction pulsing between her and Will. It had been present during the drive to the restaurant in the downtown district of Allentown, and had simmered between them all through dinner. She grasped the long stem of her glass and looked directly into Will's eyes.

"Tommy is really spending the whole night at Stephanie's?" he asked softly.

He'd been this way all through dinner. Sultry and warm and more than a little brash, his words had said one thing, and his tone something else entirely.

Swirling her wine, she said, "I wasn't sure what to do about the fact that he wanted to sleep over at her house tonight. I talked to Stephanie's mother, and neither of us can see any harm in a six- and seven-year-old camping out in the living room."

A smile pulled at his lips. The flickering light from the candle cast a golden glow over his clean-shaven face. It brought out the highlights in his honey-colored hair and deepened the color of his eyes to a midnight blue.

Speaking softly, he said, "They'll probably be embarrassed about it five years from now. And five years after that, Tommy will probably tell all his friends that he was only six years old the first time he ... you know, slept with a girl."

Krista's eyes flew open. "They're not sleeping together! They're in separate sleeping bags in a tent on the floor."

"I highly doubt that Tommy will mention that."

For a full five seconds, she merely stared, tongue-tied, at the man sitting across from her, a man whose eyes were widened with false innocence. "Please," she finally said. "I don't want to even think about my little boy going to bed and ... you know."

When he spoke again, his voice was deeper, huskier. "What about you, Krista? Do you ever think about going to bed and ... you know?"

The candle flickered in its wax, casting shadows across his face, accentuating the planes and hollows of his features. The grin had left his mouth, but he couldn't disguise the smile in his eyes. Or the desire.

She placed her glass on the table and took her napkin from her lap. Meeting his gaze over the top of the candle, she whispered, "I'm thinking about it right now."

She'd spoken so low that Will had felt the words as much as heard them. They strummed down his body, as provocative as scented oil on feminine hands. He couldn't have moved if his life had depended upon it.

"Are you ready?" she asked.

Her question finally broke into his trance. He nodded, and watched as she rose out of the high-backed chair, so lithe and graceful that it nearly took his breath away. Her dress made a swishing sound as it settled around her legs, once again reminding him of a satin gown fluttering to the floor. Will wanted to kiss her senseless, to find a secluded place where he could lower that dress from her shoulders and expose the soft skin underneath.

He grasped his cane with one hand and reached for her fingers with the other. He didn't answer her question with words, but he hoped she saw the answer in his eyes and felt it in his touch. He was ready. And waiting.

During the ride back to Coopersburg, the full moon seemed to cast a silver glow over everything it touched. Or, Will thought to himself, maybe it was the anticipation of what was to come that had done that. It was as if all these past months of frustration, these past weeks of anticipation, had led him to this point in time, to this place with this woman.

He started the car, being careful as he backed from his parking space. "You choose the radio station," he said as he pulled out onto the one-way street.

She punched a button, and a soft twangy love ballad filled the quiet. "I didn't know you liked country music," he declared.

"It's more of an acquired taste," she answered with a wry grin. "Gina loves it, and whenever we go anywhere, it's what we listen to."

"Have you ever listened to a country song backward?" he asked.

Krista rolled her eyes. "I know, I know. He gets his dog back. He gets his house back. He gets his wife back. Honestly, Will, that's Gina's worst joke."

They laughed together. When the lights of a passing vehicle momentarily illuminated the interior of the car, their gazes met, and their laughter trailed away. Will accelerated the car and reached for her hand.

Several songs played over the radio in succession, each one marking another set of miles, each mile taking them closer to their destination. "We're here," she whispered when he pulled into her driveway.

She'd left the porch light on, but all the windows were dark. Will could hardly wait to get inside. The fifteen-minute drive to Coopersburg had taken twelve minutes. Twelve of the longest and most anticipation-filled minutes of his life. He was glad he'd found a restaurant in Allentown and not in Philadelphia. He was certain he'd never have survived an hour-long drive from there.

Krista felt inside her purse for her key, then reached for the handle on the door. They met at the front of his car and strode into the house together. "I could brew a pot of coffee if you'd like," she said.

His cane thunked quietly on the floor as he came to lean against the counter next to her. "Do you remember the night you told me that coffee is your one and only weakness?"

The sound of his smooth, deep voice heated her most secret places. She slid out of her coat and looked up into his eyes, the dim light over the stove casting half his face in shadow. Reaching a hand to his cheek, she slowly drew his face toward hers. "I think I already knew that wasn't true, Will. You've always been my strongest weakness."

Their eyelids lowered little by little as their faces drew closer. Even in her three-inch heels, she had to go up on her tiptoes to get as close to him as she wanted to be. He angled his chin down for better access, and her eyes fluttered all the way shut.

The moment before her lips would have met his, he turned his head slightly, and her kiss missed its mark. She kissed the line in one cheek instead, then trailed two more along the corner of his lips.

It had been years since she'd kissed a man, years since she'd wanted to. A little out of practice, she levered her other hand on his chest. Relying on instinct, she fitted her body tight to his. His hardness pressed into her stomach and she automatically moved against him, moving her lips toward his at the same time. She heard his sharp intake of breath, but it wasn't until her lips missed his a second time that she started to get suspicious.

He wasn't really going to wait to kiss her until she asked, was he?

He let out a low moan, his hands moving to cup her hips. Emboldened by his masculine sound, she let her eyes flutter open dreamily, her gaze trailing from his pouty lips to his eyes.

Oh, yes he was.

"Aren't you forgetting something?" he whispered huskily, his mouth a mere hairbreadth away from hers.

His hands moved over her backside, fitting her to the hard contours of his body. He trailed his fingers up her back, following the line of her ribs to the skin at her sides. She stopped breathing when he skimmed the outer swells of her breasts, stopped thinking when he took them in his large hands.

Her head fell back. She brought it up again, intent upon only one thing. She had to join her mouth to his, to feel his lips against hers, to connect with this man who took her breath away.

"Uh, uh, uh," he whispered.

It took a moment for those three little syllables to make their way into her consciousness. It took a moment longer for her to understand what they meant.

When he'd whispered those words before, they'd been playful. There was nothing playful about them tonight. She could hear the strain in his voice, could feel it in the tenseness of his muscles. He wanted this as much as she did. There was one annoying problem.

She moved her hips against his, and almost forgot what else she was going to do. Raising up on tiptoe, she glided her hands to either side of his face. Closer she came, and closer still.

"I always knew you were stubborn," she whispered, steadying his face between her hands.

"It's a gift," he answered, his mouth close to hers, almost touching, but not quite.

This had gone on long enough.

"Kiss me, dammit," she whispered.

"Oh, Krista," he said, fitting his hand to the back of her neck. "I thought you'd never ask."

His lips captured hers. Suddenly. Finally. All the pent-up emotion, all the waiting, all the desire that had pulsed between them melded in that one kiss. Hotter than anything either of them had ever known, the joining of their mouths only intensified their passion.

Blood pounded in Will's brain and sensations spiraled in every direction. Her hands were everywhere, and so were his. Their breathing became sporadic, the sounds they made heady. For all Will knew, he could have died and gone to heaven. Her tongue glided into his mouth, and need jolted to a place that was already throbbing for attention.

People made love on kitchen counters in the movies, but he wanted Krista in bed. Tearing his mouth from hers, he pressed his face into her hair. "There's one room in this house you haven't shown me. Show it to me now?"

She somehow managed to untangle her arms and legs from his. Casting him a tremulous smile that went straight to his head, she took his hand and led him into the living room and down the short hall.

He opened her door with his cane and didn't stop until he reached her bed. Light from the streetlamp outside flickered through the woven shades like stardust, illuminating their way. For weeks he'd known she was the star he was reaching for. He reached for her now.

Spreading his fingers into her hair, he quickly did away with the pins, letting them drop to the carpet below. After sliding his suit coat from his broad shoulders, she worked the knot of his tie loose and unfastened the buttons on his shirt. Using one hand to steady himself with his cane, he lowered the zipper at her back with the other. When she winsomely raised both her hands to unfasten her necklace, he couldn't look away.

She dropped the necklace to the nightstand and moved to slide a dangling earring from her ear. "Leave them," he whispered. "All night long I've been thinking about how they'll feel brushing against my skin."

She combed her fingers through her hair and let her dress slide from her shoulders. Her slip went next, then her nylons and shoes. Will had to sit to remove his clothes. Instead of making him feel awkward, Krista's hands were suddenly there, sliding the Italian leather from his feet, moving her fingers up his calves, past his knees, to the closure on his pants.

She covered him with her hand, her eyes glittering into his. "You're going to pay for forcing me to *ask* you to kiss me." With a laugh he'd always found sexy as hell, she gently pushed him back onto the bed.

"Go ahead, Krista," he whispered huskily. "Do what you have to do. We both know I deserve it."

She lowered his zipper and eased his pants from his body. His shirt, socks and briefs came next. Will doubted he deserved what she did after that. Even the greatest saint didn't deserve the kind of heaven she gave him with her hands, her mouth and her body.

Krista wasn't shocked at her eager response to the man in her arms. Nothing about tonight was shocking, not this golden wave of passion, not their whispered caresses, not her sharp intakes of breath or the fire spreading to her innermost places.

As if he couldn't stand another moment of her ministerings, Will suddenly rolled her onto her back and covered her body with his. For a man who had been injured four months ago, he had incredible stamina. He caressed and touched and kissed. If his legs wouldn't cooperate completely, he improvised. The man, she realized in a haze of passion, was extremely inventive.

As his hands roamed intimately over her breasts and down to the curve of her stomach, and farther, she pulled in a deep breath, a pleasurable moan escaping her parted lips. He kissed and laved and suckled until she writhed beneath him, out of control. The next thing she knew, she was sprawled on top of him.

He saw to protection, his caresses growing in urgency, matching her need, a need that quivered inside her, a need that one thing, and one thing only, could satisfy. He fitted her to him so quickly that she gasped. Adjusting to him, she began to move, her breathing as lusty, her needs as unabated, as his.

"Ah, Will," she chanted as the fiery sensations started low in her body, building with every movement, until she moaned out loud with erotic pleasure. When his movements became even more intense, they reached for the stars together and went bursting to the other side of midnight.

It seemed like a long time before they came back down to earth. Will pulled her down on top of him, fitting her curves tight to his body. They stayed that way while their breathing became normal, and the room stopped spinning.

A short time later, she whispered, "Do you want to spend the night?"

"You mean sleep over?"

She raised her head to look at him. He winked broadly and she said, "You're hopeless."

"Maybe, but you're incredible. And yes, I'd like to spend the night with you, Krista. I'd like that very much."

Except for the times when Tommy had been frightened by storms, she'd slept alone in her double bed every night. It had been years and years since she'd exchanged pillow talk with a man. They shimmied under the covers and suddenly with her head resting on one pillow and Will's on another she felt a little afraid. Now that he'd reminded her how wonderful intimacy could be, she'd never want to do without it again.

"Tired?" he asked.

She could make out the outline of his face and shoulder in the darkness. A little relieved that he couldn't see her right now, she said, "A little. Are you?"

"I'm damned exhausted. That's what I am. I feel like I've just run around all four bases at breakneck speed. But honestly, Krista, I've never felt better."

She smiled at his humor and went into his arms when he reached for her, resting her head on his chest. "You mention baseball often, Will. Are you sure you're ready to give it up?"

"I'm sure."

Her eyelashes fluttered down and back up again. "How did your friends take the news?"

She nearly stretched like a cat in the sun when his hand stroked up and down her back. "They weren't too happy about it. They told me not to tell the press yet, in case I change my mind. I can't believe they're really so surprised."

"People associate Billy the Kid with baseball," she said softly. "It's what you always wanted to do. It's the reason you left eight years ago."

"Krista?" he asked, his breath moving her hair. "Why didn't you go with me back then?"

She closed her eyes, answering on a sigh. "Because you didn't ask."

For a moment Will held his breath. She hadn't beaten around the bush. As usual, her honesty gave him pause and made him think. "Would you have gone with me if I had asked?" he whispered.

Her hair tickled Will's chin when she nodded.

Her breathing grew steady and even; Will was pretty sure she was falling asleep. His hand on her back gradually stilled, but his thoughts wouldn't rest.

He loved her. Shock wedged the words in his throat, making it impossible to utter them out loud. He loved her. And yet he'd left her eight years ago when she would have gone with him if only he'd asked. He'd been a fool back then. Watching the light flicker through the shades like stardust, he vowed not to be a fool again.

Glorious.

Long before he came out of a deep sleep, Will realized he felt downright glorious. He awoke gradually, unable to remember why he felt so wonderful. It had something to do with stardust, and with long, dangling earrings.

His eyes opened. His lips lifted. Ah, yes, stardust and long dangling earrings. And Krista.

His passion was already beginning to rouse just thinking about her. God, he couldn't wait to see her, to touch her, to... Being careful not to wiggle the bed too much, he rolled over and found her side of the bed empty. Disappointed, he looked up at the ceiling and then at his watch. It was only seven-thirty. Where was she?

Listening intently, he couldn't hear water running, and ruled out the possibility that she was taking a shower. He tucked one hand under his head and breathed deeply, pulling the aroma of fresh coffee all the way to the bottom of his lungs. Coffee. Of course, she claimed she couldn't begin her day without it. He would have preferred that she begin her day with him.

As far as Will knew, she hadn't even liked coffee back in college. Since then she'd developed a taste for country music, too. She'd changed in the most subtle of ways these past eight years. Eight years. It looked as if he had a lot of time to make up for.

Sitting up, he made a quick inspection of her room. It had been too dark to see last night, but today, with the morning light filtering through the lace shades, it was exactly the way he'd expected Krista's bedroom to be. Feminine without being frilly, it was decorated in muted shades of blue and beige. The headboard was made out of bamboo, the chair in the corner wicker.

Their clothes were still scattered from the door to the bed. Will smiled again as he remembered how impatient they'd been to remove them. His dark suit was going to have to be professionally pressed. He wouldn't care if it was wrinkled beyond repair. He had other suits in his closet, but he and Krista had only had one night of passion. One night in eight years.

Reaching for his cane, he hurried into the adjoining bathroom. Minutes later he pulled on his dress pants, leaving the rest of his clothes on the floor. He'd considered showering, but had decided he'd rather wait until Krista showered with him. Just the thought of soaping up her lush body brought his need back with incredible force.

Following the scent of fresh coffee, he quietly made his way from the room, not stopping until he'd reached the kitchen doorway. Krista was standing in front of the coffeemaker, her back to him. Her hair waved past her shoulders, the sash of her long periwinkle robe cinched tight around her waist. The daffodils he'd given her Friday night sat on the windowsill in the bay window, blooming in the morning sunshine. It was past the middle of November, but suddenly it felt like spring.

"You're up early."

Krista turned at the sound of Will's deep voice. His chest and feet were bare, his dress slacks zipped but not buttoned. Her heart went soft and her body warmed just from the sight of him standing in her kitchen.

"Tommy's turned me into an early riser," she said, suddenly feeling shy. "I was just thinking about starting breakfast."

"That isn't what I was thinking about starting just now. What would you like?"

His question hung in the air between them like dust motes floating on a ray of sunshine. "For breakfast?" she asked, all feminine innocence.

"That, too," he answered, his voice dipping as low as it could go.

The coffee sputtered as water dripped through the filter. "Would you like a cup of coffee?" she asked.

"If you're having one," he answered, walking closer.

She poured steaming coffee into two mugs.

"Krista, are you nervous?" When she didn't readily answer, he reached for her hand. "How could you possibly be nervous with me after last night? I mean, *that* was downright therapeutic."

She finally looked up at him and shook her head. "You're something else, do you know that?"

"It's this grin. I'm told it's beguiling."

She studied his lips thoroughly before saying, "I'd call it more endearing than beguiling."

Endearing, huh? Will liked the sound of that.

He took a step closer, his knee brushing against her satin gown. His arousal was growing heavy, his voice husky as he said, "Since I'd hate to hurt your beautiful skin with my day-old beard, I thought about shaving and snooped in your medicine cabinet. I'm afraid I draw the line at using a purple razor designed exclusively for a woman's legs."

His humor worked magic over Krista, chasing her nerves away. Rubbing her palm across his cheek, she said, "That's okay. I'd hate to see you nick that adorable little dimple in your chin."

"You think I'm adorable?"

He'd stepped closer, his arousal pressing into her stomach. Suddenly, the word *adorable* no longer seemed fitting. Reaching her hand between their bodies, she whispered, "You know exactly what I think."

He made a sound deep in his throat as her hand closed partway around him. "Ah, yes," he said on a shudder. "I've always known that you have a dirty mind. I wouldn't have it any other way."

"You and Tommy," she said with a shake of her head.

"What time is he coming home?"

"Ten o'clock."

"Ten o'clock?" he mused aloud. "That should give us just about enough time."

For the second time in a matter of hours, passion wrapped around them like a cloud as they walked down to Krista's bedroom. Clothes were discarded and a shower burst on. Later, a mattress shifted, and lovers sighed. In the kitchen, the clock on the stove ticked, and two mugs of steaming coffee slowly cooled.

"What do you think of this one?" Gina asked, holding up a silver nightgown so light and airy it looked like moonlight.

"I think it's lovely," Krista answered, smiling at her friend's excitement.

"I don't know," Gina persisted. "I've always had a passion for red."

Gina and her husband, Taylor, were going on a romantic overnight getaway, the first since before the triplets had been born nearly two years ago. Gina had roped Krista into helping her shop for evening wear.

"Come on, Krista," Gina cajoled. "Why don't you surprise Will with one of these?"

Glancing all around her, Krista said, "Actually, Will prefers me in nothing at all."

"One of those guys," Gina answered knowingly. "Oh well, just think about all the money you'll save on lingerie."

It had been a week since she and Will had eaten dinner at that French restaurant, a week since Will had spent the night with her. He'd come over almost every night since. As soon as Tommy went to sleep, he'd taken her into his arms and taken her to heaven. But because of Tommy, he hadn't spent the night again, and her bed had never seemed lonelier.

After a few more minutes of careful deliberation between the silver nightgown and a red one that made Gina's face look as pale as alabaster and her skin the color of rich cream, her friend said, "I still think you should try one of these nightgowns. The first time Will sees you in one of these little numbers he'll feel as if he's been hit between the eyes."

"I don't think so, Gina."

"How do you know?"

"Because," Krista answered. "The only thing that's ever hit him between the eyes is a line drive from home plate. His life is going through so many changes right now, what with the accident and his decision not to return to baseball. He probably doesn't even know which end is up, let alone how he feels about me."

"Do you know how you feel about him?" Gina asked.

"I love him. I never stopped."

"Krista, you have to tell him. Taylor and I almost didn't make it because neither of us could say those three little words. Buy one of those little teddies over there and tell him."

"One of those little things? I don't think so. You're tall enough and svelte enough to carry one off. I'm not."

"I don't know, Krista. Small packages can sometimes be even more powerful."

"Name one."

"Well, there's the atom bomb."

"I don't want him to explode, Gina. I just want him to love me."

"So tell him first."

"I told him I loved him lots of times eight years ago and it didn't change anything. He still left. I'll know he loves me if he asks me to share his life this time."

"If you leave town I'm going to miss you," Gina sniffed, holding a garnet-colored wisp of satin to her breast.

"He hasn't asked me to go anywhere with him yet."

"He will. If he knows what's good for him, he will. Now, what do you think, the red one or the silver one?"

Krista looked at each of the gowns in Gina's hands before casting her friend a wry grin. "The red one," they said together. "Definitely the red one."

Nine

"Do you think he's really asleep this time?" Will whispered, afraid to make a sound lest Tommy came up with another excuse not to call it a night.

Krista crossed her fingers on both hands. "I think so, but I thought that an hour ago."

Will smiled, fighting a losing battle to bank his desire. Krista had been trying to get Tommy to go to sleep for an hour and a half. The fact that it was a school night had made absolutely no difference whatsoever to the little tyke. Neither had bribes from Will. For a while there, he'd thought the kid would never nod off.

"If he calls one of us in there again, I'm taking him for a long drive," he whispered in feigned exasperation.

"You're a fast learner."

"I can be slow when I want to be." He took her hands in his, placing them on his chest, encouraging her to explore.

"We're going to have to be quiet, in case Tommy isn't sleeping soundly yet," she whispered, her eyes telling him something completely different than her words.

His chest heaved with the deep breath he took, and her hands moved gently down his chest, skimming his waist, exploring lower as if they had a mind of their own. Within seconds, Will was pretty sure *he* didn't have a mind at all.

"Ah, Krista?" he murmured huskily. "I'll try to be quiet, but when you touch me like that, it isn't easy."

Her lashes were thick and dark and cast shadows on her cheeks every time she blinked. She was wearing a thin black blouse that scooped low in the front and a long airy skirt in a fabric as light as a breeze. The material skimmed beneath his hand, gliding over her warm skin underneath.

"I haven't heard a peep out of Tommy in quite a while," he whispered, his lips trailing along her cheek, over the gold-studded earring in her lobe, and on to her jaw. "Let's go to your bedroom where we can lock the door and I can help you out of your clothes."

"You don't like my outfit?" she whispered, brushing her lips provocatively against his.

"I love it. Every time I saw your blouse ripple against your breasts tonight, every time that skirt swished into place around your legs, all I could think about was touching what was underneath."

He touched her now, through the thin fabric, watching as her head tipped back and her eyes closed and opened again. She smiled a knowing smile as she said, "Gina tried to talk me into buying a sexy nightgown last week, but I told her you preferred me in nothing."

She twined her fingers through his and sashayed into her bedroom. Will followed a step behind, closing the door without making a sound and deftly sliding the lock into place. She'd told her best friend about him. He supposed that was a start, but she hadn't said a word to anyone at work. Keeping his feelings hidden at the rehab center was becoming increasingly difficult. He wasn't sure how much longer he could refrain from kissing her there, and touching her, and shouting at the top of his lungs that she was the best thing that had ever happened to him.

Thank goodness he didn't have to keep his feelings hidden here. Here, he could look into her eyes and kiss her full lips and deftly free the buttons down the front of her blouse. Here, he could touch her and hold her and make love with her as if there were no tomorrow.

"Then I was right?" she asked softly. "You really don't like sexy lingerie?"

"Just wrappings," he said huskily, his hands sliding inside her open blouse. "Beautiful wrappings. I always tore into my Christmas presents, ripping the paper to shreds. My mother swore I never noticed what was on the outside."

Krista's breasts surged into the palm of Will's hands, her lacy bra all that was between his flesh and hers. "Does that mean you don't notice what's on the outside of me?" she asked. A low moan escaped her lips as he worked the front closure of her bra free and whisked the garment away.

"Oh, I notice," he whispered, his husky voice luring her closer as his hands pressed along her back, fitting her tight to his body and crushing her breasts to his chest. Pulling away enough to look into her eyes, he said, "Believe me, I like what I see, and what I feel. But what's on the inside of you, Krista—now that's truly magnificent."

His words worked over her like a kiss, stealing inside her thoughts and her body. For a moment, she stood perfectly still, reveling in the knowledge that he liked her for what she was, who she was. Eight years ago she thought she'd loved him as much as a woman could love a man. She'd been wrong.

Krista reached a hand to either side of his face, slowly drawing him to her. The time for talking was over. She twined her hands around his neck and raised on tiptoe to join her lips with his. He sank to the edge of the bed, but as usual, he didn't take his lovemaking sitting down. He wrapped his arms around her waist and leaned back until they were lying down.

The light of a dim lamp penetrated the darkness, washing the entire room in a golden glow. Her skirt swished to the floor, his jeans following close behind. Briefs and panties came next, until it was just Will and Krista, man to woman, skin to skin, heart to heart.

One minute, his touch was like the softest waterfall, sending sensations cascading down her body. The next, his hands moved over her in a frenzy, as demanding and passionate and lusty as a cyclone, stirring up quivering sensations everywhere he touched.

Her breasts were round and full. For years, she'd been convinced *they* were the only reason men gave her a second look. Will paid close attention to her breasts, kneading and caressing and suckling, but he was even more interested in her pleasure. No one had ever made her feel the way he did, as if her breasts were a part of a whole, a whole he found beautiful and awe-inspiring and perfect in every way.

He hadn't said a word about the future, their future, but as Will worked his own special magic on her body, she drew breath into her lungs and exhaled on a sigh. He *had* to love her. No one could take so much care to bring her pleasure to take her to such incredible heights without loving her. One of these days, he'd tell her. One of these days, he'd ask her to share his life. For now, she had to be content to share this moment.

She found herself on her back, gazing into the darkest blue eyes she'd ever seen. "I want you," he confessed, his mouth inches from hers.

"Then take me," she answered, luring him closer with her tongue, sharing with him one of the French things they both loved.

The kiss spun out of control, their bodies rising and falling in undulating motions, until Krista called out to him to come to her. He joined them together then, and their passion built, fulfilling a searing need, the need of a man for a woman, and a woman for a man. Just when she thought it would never end, she cried out in release, and Will soon followed.

Krista clung to his shoulders as she floated back down to earth. *Tell me you love me,* she whispered inside her head. *Tell me you want me in your life.*

A smile found its way to her lips as she thought of all the ways he'd loved her this past week. It seemed that Will Sutherland was more of a show than tell kind of guy.

Be patient, she told herself. *As patient as he was when he waited for you to ask him for a kiss.* Krista could be patient. She could wait. She'd already waited eight years. A few more days or weeks wouldn't matter, not really. Especially when Will was reaching for her again.

"Look at you! You're walking!"

"Cort!" Will exclaimed, opening the door wide. "What are you doing here?"

Cort Sutherland shouldered his way past him and turned around. "Geez, Will," he admonished. "Can't a person drop in on his brother without needing a reason?"

Will closed his apartment door and eyed his brother's self-confident swagger. "Of course," Will said. "Just because you showed up out of the blue and landed on my doorstep before noon on a weekday is no cause for alarm."

"I knew you'd see it my way," Cort agreed with lazy charm.

Cort was a year and a half younger than Will. His hair was a little darker, but they had similar builds and shallow dimples in their chins that were dead ringers for their father's. They'd been close all their lives, but Will happened to know that his only brother never left Nebraska without an awfully good reason.

"Mom sent you, didn't she?"

Cort tried shrugging first. When that didn't work, he turned that old Sutherland grin loose and said, "It's supposed to be a secret mission, but you know her too well."

"When I talked to her last weekend, I told her everything was fine," Will grumbled.

Cort pushed a newspaper and a wrinkled sweatshirt off the couch and cast his brother a sardonic look. Will waited until Cort had settled his frame into the couch and had propped his feet on the marble coffee table to ask, "What's Mom worried about this time?"

"You know her. When *she* got cold she made *us* put on a sweater. She was concerned when you didn't come home for Thanksgiving. She said you sounded preoccupied when she talked to you last weekend and she's just sure there's something wrong. Your manager's been calling, too. He says you're depressed and thinking about giving up baseball. You don't look depressed to me, so it must involve a woman."

Deciding to ignore Cort's reference to *a woman,* Will said, "Harowitz is really calling out at the ranch?"

"Are you really thinking about giving up baseball?"

When it came to persistence, Will and Cort had always gone neck and neck all the way to the finish line. "Yes, Cort, I am. Baseball players are traded like marbles. I'm almost thirty-one years old. For a pro athlete, that's practically over the hill. Most of the guys I started with have already retired for one reason or another. I was going to have to quit sooner or later, anyway. That accident forced me to take a long hard look at my life a little sooner, that's all."

"And while you were looking, you saw this woman you mentioned earlier."

"I didn't mention Krista. You did," Will answered, falling right into Cort's trap.

"Ha!" Cort shouted, slapping his knee. "I knew there had to be a woman. You're wearing new jeans and I caught a whiff of your after-shave the minute you opened the door. Another Krista, huh?"

"There's only one Krista for me, Cort." While realization dawned on his brother, Will strode to the armchair, sat down and balanced his cane against his knee.

Cort shrugged out of his leather coat and pushed up his sleeves. "At least one of us Sutherland men hasn't lost his touch with women."

"I heard about Alyssa."

Cort's expression stilled and grew serious. Will didn't say anything until one corner of his brother's mouth finally twisted upward.

"Mom," they said in unison.

"So, when are you going to bring Krista around?" Cort asked.

"There's a little problem," Will answered seriously.

"Uh-oh," Cort grumbled. "Why does it seem that with a woman, there always is? All right, tell me what gives."

"The problem isn't with her, it's with me. I hurt her, deeply, eight years ago. She's beginning to trust me, but I don't want to mess up again. Plus, she has a six-year-old son."

Cort let out a long whistle. "Does she know you love her?"

"I've shown her every way I know how."

"Then what's the problem?"

"The problem is this," Will replied. "I'd like to ask her to spend the rest of her life with me. But I can't do that until I know what I'm going to spend the rest of my life doing."

"What do you want to do?"

Will leveled his gaze at his brother. He couldn't look at Cort without thinking about the ranch with its whitewashed buildings and fences. He couldn't think about the ranch without imagining Krista there with him.

"I've been thinking about coming back to the ranch."

He watched Cort's reaction. Carefully gauging his brother's response, Will rushed on. "Aside from a few months here and there, I know it's been just you and Dad ever since I left for college. I wouldn't expect either of you to step aside for me, but I have two strong hands and I always loved working the fields and—"

"Would you shut up?" Cort cut in.

Will's head jerked up a notch and his shoulders tensed.

"I can't believe you'd even think—" Cort paused for a moment "—you'd have to ask. That ranch is as much yours as it is mine."

Will felt his jaw go slack a moment before a grin found its way to his entire face. Cort continued talking, while Will tried to listen. "We just bought another four hundred acres, and Dad's not as young as he used to be, although if you tell him I said that I'll deny it with my dying breath. We could definitely use another pair of strong hands, especially if those hands are yours. Yee-ha! It looks as if the Sutherland brothers are going to be back together again."

Will grinned sheepishly and shook his head. It wasn't long before he was laughing right along with Cort.

He pictured the ranch in his mind. It was early December, and any day now it would start to snow. He and Cort had grown up there, and their childhoods had been pretty darned close to perfect. It would be a great place to raise Tommy. After he convinced Krista to marry him and move to Nebraska with him, he wouldn't mind getting started having a little baseball team of their own. The very idea made him feel downright lofty.

He remembered her response when he'd asked why she didn't go with him eight years ago. *"Because you didn't ask."*

This time, he was going to ask. Will could hardly wait.

"How long are you staying?" he asked Cort.

"A couple of days."

"Good," Will began, anticipation growing inside him like a balloon. "That'll give us a little time to catch up, and still give me enough time to sweep one special woman off her feet.''

"You've got a plan, haven't you?" Cort asked, his eyes narrowing, his grin matching Will's.

"As a matter of fact I do, Cort. I sure do."

"Surprise!"

Krista watched as Mrs. A turned in a complete circle, her blue eyes twinkling at each and every patient, therapist and friend. "We're going to miss you," Heather said.

"Yeah," Brody agreed. "This place won't be the same without you."

"Oh, fiddle faddle," Mrs. A replied. "You're going to miss beating me in poker. That's what you're going to miss, young man."

"Did you hear that everybody?" Brody asked loudly. "She called me a *young* man."

Krista laughed along with everyone else. Mrs. A—Violet—was going home at the end of the week, and everyone in the entire wing had taken their afternoon break together to gather for her going-away party. Someone let go of a bunch of balloons. Someone else tossed a handful of confetti.

Peering between Heather and Brody, Krista felt a smile steal over her as she met Will's coy wink. His blue eyes crinkled beneath dark brows and a cockily masculine grin stole across his face. He'd made such incredible progress at the Fourth Street Rehab Center that his physical therapy was officially over. He'd hired a personal trainer to help him with building up the strength in his legs, and another patient had filled his two-hour time slot between ten and noon. He still woke up with a cup of coffee every morning and did four miles on the treadmill at the end of the day. Life tended to go on, but Krista felt as if she'd been forever changed.

Now that Will wasn't her patient anymore, she was going to tell the people here at the rehab center that she loved him.

Just as soon as he told her he wanted her in his life, or at least gave her some little sign. If the glint in his eyes was an accurate indication, she didn't think it was going to be much longer now.

He'd seemed even loftier than usual when he'd called her this afternoon, more cocky and excited. He'd asked her what she was doing tonight. As usual, his words said one thing, his tone something else entirely. She'd told him she had an appointment to get her hair trimmed, but the way his voice had warmed her thoughts, she'd thought about canceling.

"How long will that take?" he'd asked.

"About an hour," she'd replied.

"Then go," he'd returned. "I'll come over to stay with Tommy. There's something I want to do, and he can help."

"What's that?"

"I'd rather show you than tell you," he'd insisted, his voice dipping low, taking her thoughts all the way to the bedroom and back again.

Yes, Will Sutherland was definitely a show rather than tell kind of guy. He had something up his sleeve, and she could hardly wait to find out what it was.

The sound of laughter and raised voices drew her back to the present. She looked on as Tommy and Stephanie made their way, hand in hand, to talk to Violet.

Tommy had been thrilled to have the opportunity to actually meet Mrs. A. Even though he was beginning to talk about the other boys in his class, it was Stephanie he'd asked to come with him today. Krista didn't know what her son was going to say to her sprightly friend, but she was quite sure it would have something to do with elves and the North Pole. Tommy believed in Christmas magic, and when his eyes met Will's a second time, so did she.

"Come on," Stephanie whispered to Tommy. "Let's ask her if your Christmas wishes are all going to come true."

"I don't know, Stephanie," Tommy said. "I don't think we're supposed to ask. I think we're just supposed to believe."

"Of course we can ask. When Mr. Abernathy lived in my apartment building, I used to talk to him about my Christmas wishes, and they still came true."

"Hello, Tommy, Stephanie."

Two pairs of brown eyes rounded with childish wonder as the children turned around. "You remember our names?" Tommy asked shyly.

"Of course she does," Stephanie whispered. "Mr. and Mrs. Santa Claus remembers everybody's name."

"Cool."

"Are you really leaving at the end of the week?" Stephanie asked.

"Yes, dear, I am. There are only fourteen days until Christmas, and even though everything is computerized these days, I'm afraid Nicholas and the boys are going to snap if I don't lend them a hand soon. Besides, I miss them terribly."

"How old are your boys?" Tommy asked.

"Nicholas Jr. is forty-two. Noel is thirty-seven, and Chris is thirty-five."

Stephanie giggled behind her hand. "They're not boys. They're men."

Mrs. A winked at her and said, "One day you're going to have a son of your own. Then you'll understand."

"I'm going to have a little boy someday?" Stephanie asked shyly.

"One of each, I believe," Mrs. A said matter-of-factly.

"Do you suppose that Tommy is going to get all his Christmas wishes, Mrs. A?"

Tommy followed Mrs. A's gaze straight to Will. Before Mrs. A could answer, he whispered, "He's the father I asked for, isn't he?"

"Yes, Tommy, I believe he is," she answered.

Tommy and Stephanie both shrieked with excitement. Throwing their arms around Mrs. A's ample waist, neither of them saw the worry lining her forehead as she looked from Will to Krista, and back again.

"Just remember, Tommy," she said seriously. "Keep on wishing with everything you have. The magic of Christmas is in the believing." With that, she turned around, hurrying toward the center of the room.

"Mrs. A?" Stephanie called in a voice so tiny Tommy didn't see how the older lady would ever hear.

As if by magic, Mrs. A turned around again.

"Would you tell Mr. Abernathy I said hi? When you get back to the North Pole, I mean."

A tear twinkled in Mrs. A's eye, reminding Tommy of a snowflake melting in the sunshine. "Of course, dear. I'll tell him. And I'm sure he sends his love."

Tommy and Stephanie stared at each other for a long moment. This time they both said, "Cool."

The V-8 engine practically purred as Will pulled around the last corner. He was driving his own car tonight, a shiny midnight blue sports car with four on the floor and raised-letter tires. That wasn't the reason for his inner excitement. He was going to begin talking to Krista about his future, their future. He had something different planned for every night this week. Tonight he was going to spend time with Tommy. Tomorrow night he planned to take Tommy's mother out to dinner, someplace secluded and romantic and French. He'd show her over and over again that he wanted her to share his life, to be his wife, and that he intended to be a father to Tommy.

A niggling doubt had crept down his spine this afternoon when he'd seen Krista with all her friends and patients at work. They loved her, truly cared for her. For a moment he'd wondered what right he had to ask her to leave them behind. But when she looked into his eyes, he'd known th answer. Of course those people loved her. But so did he. There were rehab centers in Nebraska, and Will didn't have a doubt in his mind that she'd make just as many friends there.

Balancing all his purchases in one hand, Will grasped his cane with the other and hurried up the sidewalk. Snowflakes were starting to sift down from the sky. The beginning of winter had never felt so much like the beginning of spring.

Tommy threw the door open before Will could knock. Krista was suddenly there, shaking her head and breathing a sigh of relief. "Honestly, Tommy. Sometimes I worry that one of these days you're going to open this door and someone like Will won't be standing on the other side."

Will went perfectly still. Whether Krista knew it or not, she'd just paid him a high compliment, perhaps the highest he'd ever received. She trusted him. To be on the other side of the doors Tommy opened, but in other ways, too. She trusted him. He'd never felt so honored, so proud and so humble all at once. That niggling sense of doubt he'd felt earlier disappeared into thin air.

"What did you bring me?" Tommy asked, jumping up and down.

"It's a surprise for your mother. You can help me as soon as she leaves."

"You don't want to be late for your appointment, Mommy," Tommy said as if he was ten times older than his six years.

Eyeing the two males looking for all the world like cats who'd swallowed a proverbial canary, Krista felt her lips curve into a leisurely smile. She'd been doing that a lot lately, so often, in fact, that Tommy had stopped looking at her peculiarly each time it happened.

"Are you two trying to get rid of me?" she asked playfully, glancing at the paper bags in Will's arm. She was pretty sure she'd caught a glimpse of a daffodil peaking out of the top of one of them and wondered what he was up to.

"Only if you promise to come back," Will answered. "There's something I want to talk to you about when you do."

His implication sent waves of excitement through her. He wasn't smiling exactly, but the expression in his eyes was so intense it took her breath away. Krista couldn't deny the spark of desire that ignited deep inside her. Will wanted to talk to her about something important. He was finally going to tell her he loved her—she just knew it.

"All right," she said, taking her navy blue parka from the closet. "I'll leave you two men alone. But I'll be back."

"We'll be waiting," Will answered, his lips curving into that cocky grin that was the very essence of the man himself.

She leaned down to kiss Tommy on the cheek and surprised the living daylights out of Will when she reached up and did the same to his. It took incredible willpower to keep his touch on her back light or to let her slip away without pulling her closer for a more thorough kiss.

She looked back at them once, and Will and Tommy both gave her their most innocent smiles. The second the door was closed, Tommy said, "Whew, I thought she'd never leave. Now, what did you want me to help you with?"

Chuckling, Will handed one of the paper sacks to the boy, thinking that it was going to be great being this little kid's father, this little boy who really was six going on thirty. "Do you remember when I went to your classroom for show-and-tell? I'm going to apply the same principle to your mother. Come on, let's take this stuff to the kitchen table and I'll show you what I mean."

Will spread paper on the table and removed pots of blooming daffodils from his bags. The florist had thought he was crazy when he'd ordered daffodils. Requesting these little packets of seeds, too, had had the man shaking his head in confusion. As long as Krista understood what these plants meant, Will didn't care if the florist *did* think he was crazy.

Tearing open the small seed packets, he showed Tommy how deep to plant them, how to cover them loosely with soil and water them. He talked about ranching and farming the whole time, about plowing fields and planting corn and wheat, sorghum, barley and beans, about praying for rain and worrying about an early frost.

Tommy listened with rapt attention, and Will felt a growing sense of pride in this little waif. Sometime during the past two months, he'd begun to think of Tommy as *his* son. Krista wanted her child to have a normal, stable childhood. Baseball hadn't been very stable, but farming was. She didn't know that Tommy had asked for a father for Christmas, but more and more, Will was beginning to feel like the father the boy had wished for.

The phone jangled just as they finished planting the second pot. Tommy hurried to answer it, and Will marveled at how grown up the child sounded. Krista had done a good job of teaching her son manners and etiquette, at the same time encouraging him to play and have fun.

Listening with only one ear to Tommy's side of the conversation, Will could hardly wait to tell Krista how he felt. He may have been a fool eight years ago when he hadn't asked her to go with him, but he wouldn't be a fool again.

"That was Gina," Tommy declared, peering into another packet of seeds. "She and Mommy are best friends. Mommy says she doesn't know what she'd ever do without her."

That niggling doubt crept back up Will's spine. He did his best to poke it down again. "Your mother cares about a lot of people, doesn't she?"

Will stopped what he was doing to watch as Tommy pressed three tiny seeds into black soil. "*Everybody* just loves her to pieces. She says she loves me more than anything. I don't like it when she won't let me stay up late on school nights, but she lets me play in the rain if it isn't lightning in the summer, and she plays ball with me and talks to me all the time."

Smoothing down the cowlick on the top of the boy's head, Will said, "You're a lucky little kid, do you know that?"

"I know. I'm gifted."

That wasn't what Will had meant. Tommy was lucky because he had Krista for a mother.

"I know my mom worries about me," Tommy said, reaching for another clay pot of blooming daffodils. "She wants me to have a happy childhood because hers wasn't so great. She wants me to fit in, and Will, ever since you came to show-and-tell, the other boys in my class have stopped calling me baby. I think they're starting to like me."

A knot rose to Will's throat and his chest felt heavy, making it difficult to breathe. Tommy prattled on as they planted the last packet of seeds, not seeming to notice that Will had grown quiet.

A knock sounded on the back door. Will strode with Tommy to answer it. There on the other side stood Dustin Jamison, the little boy who hadn't believed that Tommy knew Billy the Kid.

"Wow!" Dustin said, his gaze trailing up Will's body as if he were a giant.

The phone rang again. Leaving the two boys talking just inside the back door, Will strode to answer it. "Wilson residence," he said in a voice shakier than he would have liked.

"Who is this?" the person on the other end trilled.

"This is Will Sutherland, a friend of the family's. Who's this?"

"Oh, hello, Will. This is Katrina."

Will thought Krista's older sister almost sounded friendly. "Krista is gone right now, Katrina, but she'll be back any minute. Can I have her call you?"

"That's all right. I'll call her a little later. I've found a special school for gifted children that she might be interested in. I know she wants Tommy to have as normal a childhood as possible—"

"Tommy seems pretty happy to me just the way he is," Will interrupted, glancing down the hall where Tommy and Dustin were still talking.

"I'm sure he is, but he's my only nephew, and I want him to have nothing but the best."

Krista's eldest sister would have been easier to deal with if her voice had been mean instead of sincere. Then he could have hung up on her. As it was he listened, that niggling doubt creeping up his spine and spreading outward with every word Katrina said.

"This school is much more *normal* than the schools Kimberly, Kendra and I attended when we were children. The teachers are wonderful, and the students can attend their regular schools part of the day and this school in the afternoon, thereby fitting accelerated classes into a more normal curriculum. It's the only school like it in the United States and it's right there in Philadelphia. Just tell Krista I called, all right?"

The back door slammed just as Will hung up the phone. Tommy skipped into the room, practically bursting with excitement. "Dustin just asked me to come to his birthday party this weekend. *All* the guys are going to be there. Pennsylvania really is a place where everyone fits in!" he exclaimed, grinning from ear to ear.

Will felt as if he'd just been kicked in the chest. Krista had taken care of Tommy for six and a half years. She'd kept him safe and made him feel secure. Now the child was making friends. For the first time, he was beginning to fit in. How could he ask Krista and Tommy to move to Nebraska with him and start all over?

Tommy talked nonstop while they placed all the pots of blooming daffodils in the bay window. Will answered in monosyllables. He remembered how lofty he'd felt an hour ago when he'd realized that Krista trusted him to be on the other side of the doors Tommy opened.

Will was beginning to understand what being a father to Tommy entailed. He thought about all the sacrifices his own parents had made so that he could play baseball. Sometimes it wasn't easy being a father, not when it meant doing what was right for the child you loved, no matter how difficult it was for the parent.

The loftiness had completely left him but nothing could change the fact that he loved Krista and Tommy more than he thought possible. There had to be a way for them all to be together. Will just had to find it.

He had just finished cleaning up the remains of dirt and had stuffed the crumpled newspapers into his bag when the back door opened and Krista walked in.

"Will, Tommy," she called. "I'm home."

Ten

Krista brushed the snow from her hair and slipped out of her coat. Usually she found it relaxing to have her hair cut and styled. Tonight she'd barely been able to sit still. She couldn't help it. Her pulse leaped with excitement. She'd seen the look in Will's eyes before she'd left, and she could hardly wait to see him again.

He had his back to her when she breezed into the kitchen. It didn't matter—she beamed at him and Tommy, anyway.

"Look!" Tommy exclaimed. "We wanted to surprise you!"

She followed her son's pointed finger to the row of blooming daffodils lining the bay window in her kitchen. "They're beautiful!" she exclaimed.

The phone rang before she could say any more. Reaching to answer it, she wondered if she was imagining the tension in Will's posture. "Oh, hello, Katrina," she said absently, her mind more on Will than on what her sister was saying.

After a few moments of conversation, she replaced the receiver.

As if in slow motion, Will finally turned around. She looked into his eyes, and the excitement dancing through her veins stopped as if someone had thrown a switch. Even with the glimmers of light reflected from above, his expression was nearly unreadable.

"What's wrong?" she asked.

Will had listened to the conversation from Krista's end, cursing Katrina's rotten timing. He'd planned to show Krista how he felt this week, and had hoped that by the weekend, she'd agree to come with him to Nebraska. This new one-of-a-kind school in Philadelphia was throwing a wrench into all his carefully laid plans.

"Nothing's wrong," he said, pulling himself together. "I heard you say that was Katrina. Did she mention that she called earlier?"

Nodding, she said, "She wants me to visit a special school for Tommy tomorrow. I don't know. I've never wanted to send him to one of those."

Krista's words eased the worry in Will's mind. Everything was going to be all right. She'd never wanted to send Tommy to a special school and probably wouldn't want to send him to one now.

"What did you tell her?" he asked.

"She sounded so sincere, as if she really thinks it would be perfect for Tommy. I doubt that, but I don't think it'll hurt to check it out, do you?"

Will supposed she was right, although he couldn't shake the feeling that he'd rather be back in rehab than visit this school with Krista. "I'll go with you if you'd like," he said quietly.

It was impossible not to react to the relief, the warmth and the genuine caring in her eyes as she said, "Oh, Will. I'd like that."

Yes, Will thought to himself. Everything was going to be all right. Tomorrow he'd go with her to see that special school, and then, after she'd reaffirmed her belief that the best place for Tommy was in a regular school, he'd do everything in his power to show her just how much he loved her.

Tommy ran to play one last computer game before bedtime, and Krista slid her arms around Will's waist. "Are you sure you're all right?" she asked, raising her face toward his.

Will's arms came around her all at once, drawing her close. "Everything's fine," he whispered huskily.

"Can you stay awhile?" she asked, her mouth close to his.

Will's hands slid up her back, over her shoulders and down again, fitting her more intimately to his own body. "Cort's staying at my place, but he isn't expecting me back for hours."

They kissed, long and lingering. When their lips parted, Krista fitted her cheek to the hollow of his shoulder, thinking there was no place in the world she'd rather be than right here with this man.

Krista put the key in the back door and stepped aside to let Tommy slip past her. The light over the stove cast a soft glow throughout the room as she strode inside. She heard Will close the door behind her, but she was almost afraid to turn around and face him. Something was wrong, terribly wrong.

He'd stayed long after Tommy had fallen asleep last night. Earlier in the evening, she'd been certain he was going to tell her he loved her. Instead of putting it into words, he'd taken her into his arms and made love to her with an intensity that bordered on desperation. She'd never experienced anything like it before, had practically come apart in his arms, melding her body to his, loving him with everything she had. She'd fallen asleep sated and secure after he'd left. Now, she couldn't shake the feeling that he was slipping through her fingertips before her very eyes.

They'd just come from the special school on the north end of Philadelphia. Will had stood at her side, asking questions as if he truly cared about Tommy's well-being. Katrina was right, the staff was wonderful, the school truly extraordinary. As she and Will and Tommy had walked through the halls, seeing everything from computer equipment to the shaded playground, she'd harbored the dream that they were a family.

"It looks like Katrina was right," Will said. "Tommy would probably be very happy at that school."

Krista wondered if she was hearing things, or if his voice really sounded forced and hollow. She'd listened to every word he said during dinner and on the drive back to Coopersburg, searching for hidden meaning, trying to understand why he seemed so...different, so quiet and withdrawn. For the life of her, she didn't understand what could have put the impassive coolness in his eyes, or the hollowness in his voice.

Tommy had bombarded him with questions, but Tommy was always full of questions, and it had never seemed to bother Will before. What was it, then?

A sound at the back door drew all their glances. "Did you hear that?" Tommy asked.

Krista and Will both turned, listening. The faint tinkling sound came again. This time it was followed by a soft yipping and a series of scratches on the door.

"Can I open it?" Tommy asked, his eyes round with curiosity.

All three of them strode to the back door. Will pulled it open, and the yipping turned to high-pitched barking.

"Look!" Tommy exclaimed, scooping a tiny black ball of fur into his arms. "It's a puppy!"

Krista stepped out into the night, looking all around. There wasn't a soul in sight, no people, no cars, nothing

The only tracks in the fresh snow were the ones they'd made a few minutes ago. There weren't even any puppy tracks. How could that be? Puppies didn't fall out of trees.

Leaning over the little dog, she stroked its tiny head, saying, "Where in the world did you come from?"

The sound of sleigh bells came again. She peered all around, but still saw nothing. Her eyes met Will's, and for a moment her heart rejoiced. But then he took a step back, both physically and emotionally, and her joy turned to disappointment.

"This is my second Christmas wish," Tommy stated, as if no further explanation was necessary.

It took Krista a moment to comprehend what Tommy had said. Shaking her head to try to clear her thoughts and tamp down her disappointment, she said, "Honey, this little puppy must be lost. We have to find his owner."

Tommy giggled as the puppy licked his neck. "Puppies don't get lost with red Christmas bows on their necks, Mommy. Besides, he has a tag. See?"

It wasn't easy to read the tag with the puppy wiggling and licking her hand, but she finally managed to make out the words on the white cardboard tag attached to the bow.

"'Merry Christmas, Tommy. May you always believe,'" she read aloud. "That's strange. Who do you think it's from?"

"Why, it's from Santa Claus, of course. Or maybe Mrs. Santa Claus. What do you think I should name him?"

As if in a daze, she said, "He's cuddly. How about Cuddles?"

"Are you kidding?" Will asked. "This isn't a poodle with a pompon on his tail. Just look at the size of his feet. He's a boy's dog. How about Rambo or Bruiser or Killer?"

For the first time since she'd walked in the door, Will's voice contained the level of teasing she'd grown accustomed to hearing. Maybe everything was still going to be all right. Maybe he'd just been tired when they'd first arrive home.

"Of course," Will added. "He's your son, and if yo want him to name the dog Cuddles, I guess it's up to you."

Any hopes she might have had that he was on the verge o telling her he loved her flew right out the window. She' obviously misjudged the excitement she'd seen in his eye last night. Hadn't she always known she was a terrible judg of character? She hadn't even suspected that Steven wa married. Why should she think she had become any mo adept at it now?

Because she loved Will, that's why. She loved him, an she wanted to believe he loved her, too.

Will saw the uncertainty behind Krista's eyes and curse himself for putting it there. His gaze strayed to the row o blooming daffodils on the windowsill, thinking about all hi high hopes for the rest of the week. By Saturday he'd ha every intention of asking her to marry him, to move wit him to Nebraska where they could build a house and fu nish it with all the textures she loved.

He glanced around her kitchen, at those daffodils and th coffeemaker, the woven place mats and the cane-backe chairs. She already had a house furnished with all the tex tures she loved. And there were no one-of-a-kind schools fo gifted children in his part of Nebraska.

Tommy's laughter as he played with the puppy was noisy testimony to the fact that Will was doing the righ thing. He couldn't ask them to follow him out to Ne braska. Tommy was making friends and that new schoo could very well be the opportunity of a lifetime. He was great kid and deserved nothing but the best.

A few minutes ago Tommy had told them that his pupp was his second Christmas wish. The ball glove had been hi first, and Will, along with the rest of the second-grade class knew he'd asked for a father, too. Casting a glance at th little tyke with the scuffed tennis shoes and worn jeans, Will figured two out of three wasn't bad.

A knot rose to his throat at the raw feelings circling his heart. He'd heard of parental sacrifice, but he'd never understood it as clearly as he did right now.

The warm hand grazing his forearm drew his gaze. "Are you sure you're all right?" Krista whispered.

No, he wasn't sure. In fact, he was almost sure he'd never be all right again. But he couldn't tell her that. Swallowing the lump in his throat, he ran a hand through his hair and said, "I guess I'm more beat than I thought. I'm telling you, my new trainer makes our old therapy sessions look like a stroll in the park. He's a tyrant. But I think he'll be effective."

"I'm glad," she murmured, as if she couldn't think of anything else to say.

"Well," he stammered. "I guess I'll be going." He had to get out of there before he pulled her into his arms and blurted out his need for her.

"Will?"

Her voice stopped him before he'd made it three steps. Turning slowly, he waited for her question.

"When you first arrived last night, you said there was something you wanted to tell me. You said it as if it was important."

Will felt the warmth in her eyes drawing him in. Hell and damnation. He hadn't asked Krista to go with him eight years ago because he hadn't loved her enough. He couldn't ask her to go with him now because he loved her and Tommy too much.

After a long silent moment, he said, "I mentioned that Cort is in town. We've done a lot of talking, a lot of planning. We called Mom and Dad from my apartment and told them the news. I'm going back to Nebraska, back to the old place. I'm leaving tomorrow."

He'd always known that Krista had an incredible inne
strength. Before his eyes, she showed him what she wa
made of, straightening her spine and squaring her shoul
ders. That didn't keep the moisture from gathering in he
eyes, or the blood from draining from her face.

He felt like a heel. Worse. But dammit, he couldn't as
her to uproot Tommy, not now. That didn't mean sh
couldn't offer. She'd asked him to kiss her a month ago
Maybe she'd ask to come along with him to Nebraska now

"You're leaving?" Tommy asked, suddenly looking u
from the floor where he was playing with the puppy. "But
thought...I mean..." Without another word, the chil
found his feet and whirled around, propelling his little bod
straight for Will. This time Will went down on his knees
wrapping his arms around Tommy and the puppy. "I lov
you, Will."

Will's gaze homed in on Krista's. *Ask, dammit. Ask.*

She stood there, watching him, her arms crossed over he
heart. Her eyes spoke volumes, but her lips didn't utter
word.

Squeezing Tommy's shoulders, he memorized the way i
felt to hold this child in his arms. "I love you, too. Don'
ever forget it. Ever."

He'd spoken to Tommy, but had looked directly int
Krista's eyes. He straightened slowly, patting Tommy an
the puppy before reaching for his coat and opening the door
"Don't forget," he said to Tommy. "Water our plants onc
a week."

He implored Krista with his look. *Ask me not to go. Be
me to take you with me.*

The teardrop slowly trailing down her face was his u
doing. He strode to her and pulled her to him, his lips mo
ing over hers with the desperation of a man clutching
lifeline in a raging river. He tore his mouth away from he
on a ragged breath. In a voice so soft he wasn't sure she'

hear, he said, "If there's ever anything you or Tommy need, call me."

And then he was gone.

Somehow she held herself together until after Tommy went to bed. Tiptoeing into his room, she checked on him for the third time in five minutes. He and Blue—the black puppy he'd named after Paul Bunyan's giant ox—were both sleeping soundly, Tommy in his single bed, and the puppy curled into a ball at his side. She wandered aimlessly through her quiet house, her arms wrapped tightly around her waist. She couldn't count how many times she'd done the same thing these past three years, how often she'd sought solace from her loneliness in the textures and muted colors in her home. For some reason, her steps stopped just inside her bedroom.

The room was dark, except for the light of the moon and stars filtering through the lace shades. Star light, star bright, she whispered in her mind.

"...I wish I may, I wish I might..."

Tears welled in her eyes, then fell silently down her cheeks. Long before the last words of the rhyme had played out in her head, her knees buckled, and she sank to the floor. Krista pressed her face into a satin pillow to quiet the sobs racking her body so that Tommy wouldn't hear. She cried for a long time, shedding salty tears that came from the bottom of her soul.

She'd thought Will loved her. She'd thought that's what his kisses, his touch, and his smiles had meant, but she'd been wrong. If he loved her, he wouldn't have left. Of all the French things he'd given her, she'd never expected him to throw her a French curve.

By the following Monday, Krista couldn't hide the circles beneath her eyes. Violet had left on Friday. Wringing her hands, she'd told Krista to keep believing, then hurried away muttering something about sisters and Santa Claus. Of course, that could have been a figment of Krista's imagination. That had been happening a lot lately. She'd lost track of how many times she'd hurried to the door, certain she'd heard Will's jaunty knock, only to close the door against the emptiness on the other side.

At work, Heather and Brody tried to include her in their bantering. In fact, everybody at the rehab center handled her with kid gloves. She thought she and Will had managed to keep their relationship from her co-workers, but evidently they'd all known. Even Mrs. Felpont shook her head and tried to smile encouragingly as she slowly pushed her walker down the hall.

Gina stopped in almost every night, and Tommy and Blue kept her entertained with their antics. Everyone was wonderful, just wonderful. Krista had never felt so sad. Not when she'd found out Steven was married, not even when Will had left her behind eight years ago. This sorrow was different. This one felt permanent, weighing her down, dogging her steps, making her feel so miserable even strangers felt sorry for her.

By the time he'd been gone a week, she'd gone over and over her relationship with Will so many times it was like a movie she'd watched a hundred times. She saw him the way he'd been when he'd first set foot in the rehab center. She remembered his cocksure comments and his slow, steady smiles, but of all her memories, the little things were the most clear. She could practically hear his laughter the first time he'd stood, and could see his face in her mind when he'd told Tommy he'd go with him to show-and-tell. She couldn't have been imagining the genuine caring in his expression.

A knock sounded on the front door. As usual, Tommy ran ahead to open it. "It's the aunts!" he called.

There stood Krista's three older sisters, all wearing cashmere coats and imported leather pumps in neutral colors. "Oh, my!" Katrina said with a gasp.

"That kind-hearted woman was right!" Kimberly added.

"She's as pale as a ghost!" Kendra agreed.

Oh, no. Not my sisters. Krista wasn't sure she could withstand their fault-finding. Not tonight. "Look," she said, her voice sounding defeated even to her own ears. "Just say whatever it is you came to say. Tell me everything I'm doing wrong and get it over with."

Looking from one sister to the next, she felt a headache coming on. She placed one hand to her temple and cast Tommy a covert glance.

Kendra, who was three years older than Krista and the second in rank, took a tentative step forward and began. "We didn't come here to tell you what you've done wrong. We came because a friend of yours showed up on each of our doorsteps yesterday."

Katrina huffed, interrupting Kendra. "She told us that our baby sister needs us, that you think we don't approve of you, that we've made you feel like a misfit in your own family."

"You're the normal one!" Kimberly, the third Wilson sister cut in.

Tommy grinned up at his mother, and Krista glanced from him to each of her sisters. "What did you say?"

"You're the normal one," Kendra and Kimberly insisted.

"I wouldn't necessarily say that," Katrina insisted. Her statement cost her a jab in the ribs from Kimberly and Kendra.

"We were child prodigies," Kimberly said, her voice softer than Krista had ever heard it. "Do you know how the dictionary defines *prodigy?*"

It was Tommy who piped up and said, "Strange or unusual."

"The thesaurus is even worse," Kendra said. "A synonym for prodigy is *freak.*"

"Why, that's ridiculous!" Krista declared. "You're beautiful and talented and intelligent."

"And so are you," Kimberly said quietly.

Krista's emotions had been so raw all week she wasn't sure she could withstand being pummelled with her sisters' kindness. She looked around the room at the three blond, svelte, blue-eyed Wilsons. She'd always known they hadn't had normal childhoods. That was why she was so insistent that Tommy's be as normal as possible, but until that moment, she hadn't realized just how much their childhoods had hurt them.

"You're extremely bright yourself," Kimberly said.

"And you have a child, a home and a career," Kendra added.

"After speaking with Will on the telephone last week, I assumed the two of you were close," Katrina said, eyeing Tommy.

Krista's head jerked around to her eldest sister. Something bothered the back of her mind, something important. Could that phone call have been the turning point in Will's behavior? Coffee. She needed coffee to think clearly. Since a love of coffee was one of the few traits she shared with her sisters, she excused herself to start a pot immediately.

Tommy came into the kitchen a few minutes later, Blue close on his heels. He took a watering can from a low cupboard and strode over to the bay window where he watered the daffodils with the punctiliousness of a chemist. "Do you think Will misses us?" he asked, his back to her.

"I'm sure he misses you a great deal, honey."

It had been a week since Will and Tommy had planted those daffodils. A few days ago, they'd begun to lose their luster. Now she noticed that some of the petals had dried up.

Will had told her daffodils reminded him of her. Looking at the faded, limp flowers right now, Krista had to agree with him. If she would have been the volatile type, she would have marched to the bay window and swept each and every one of those potted plants off the ledge in one dramatic sweep. Damn him for getting her hopes up over one little kiss. But she knew that wasn't true or fair. He hadn't gotten her hopes up. *She* had. After all, she'd asked for that kiss.

"Why didn't we go with Will to Nebraska?" Tommy asked.

"We're doing pretty well here, aren't we?" she asked, slowly walking closer. "Besides, he didn't ask."

Bits and pieces of conversation were coming from the living room, and every few seconds, the coffeemaker gurgled as steaming water filtered through the grounds. Her son watered the last plant, then turned to her. "I just know he's lonely without us, Mommy. He loves you. He loves us both."

Krista didn't know how to respond. She wanted to spare Tommy's feelings, but didn't know how to do that. How could she tell a six-year-old boy that the man he idolized had never uttered one word about love? She'd wished for a sign, anything that would indicate that Will wanted her in his life.

"I don't believe—"

"You *have* to believe!" Tommy cried out. "Mrs. A said that was the most important of all."

"I know believing is important, Tommy. But Will didn't say one word about love."

"That's because he wanted to *show* you instead of *tell* you."

Something drew her gaze to the pot closest to her. A tiny little shoot was poking up through the black dirt. Why, it almost looked like corn. Leaning closer, she inspected the next pot, and the next. Daffodils and corn. Daffodils and beans. Daffodils and wheat.

Krista went perfectly still. Will had said daffodils reminded him of her. Next to each blooming daffodil, he'd planted the crops that grew on his ranch back in Nebraska. Suddenly, she remembered how excited he'd seemed before she'd left to have her hair cut. Katrina had just reminded her of her telephone conversation with Will, when she'd told him about that one-of-a-kind school in Philadelphia. *A one-of-a-kind school that wasn't in Nebraska.* One by one, the pieces were beginning to fall into place.

She'd wished for a sign that he loved her. Her *sign* was staring her right in the face. He loved her, and he wanted her at his side, the way his wheat and corn and beans were growing side by side with her daffodils. Tommy had told her she had to believe. Hadn't she always known her son was bright?

"Tommy, I believe." In her excitement, she whisked him into her arms and twirled around the kitchen. Blue yipped at her feet, his little tail wagging as he joined in the celebration.

"What's going on in here?" Katrina asked from the kitchen doorway.

Krista set Tommy back on his feet and grinned at her sister. "Tommy and I are going for a little ride tomorrow."

"Where are you going?" Katrina asked.

"To Nebraska."

Tommy's mouth fell open and his eyes widened in awe. "This means I'm going to get my third Christmas wish."

"What wish?" Kendra asked, joining them in the kitchen.

"A father! I told the whole class at show-and-tell."

Katrina gasped, and Krista paused to catch her breath. Tommy wanted a father for Christmas? Her mind began working overtime as she recalled the way her son had looked at Will, his brown eyes trusting, his expression full of wonder and belief in Christmas magic. When she tried to speak, her voice quavered. "Did Will know you wanted *him* to be your father?" she asked, her voice hovering above a whisper.

Tommy nodded solemnly. "He told everybody that he'd be proud to be my father."

Tears welled in her eyes and her heart turned over in her chest. Will had planted corn and wheat and beans with her daffodils. He'd told the entire second-grade class that he'd be proud to be Tommy's father. Yet he hadn't told her. Hadn't she always known that Will Sutherland was more of a show than tell kind of guy?

"Tommy, I think it's time for us to *show* Will just how much we both love him, don't you?"

Glancing at her sisters, Krista said, "Tommy and I are going to Nebraska tomorrow. I think I'm going to need my three gifted sisters to be bridesmaids in my wedding."

Kimberly and Kendra smiled through their tears. For a moment Katrina seemed at a loss for something to say. Recovering her voice, she said, "Promise you won't ask us to wear pink taffeta with ruffles and lace. Ow!" she sputtered, rubbing her arm where Kimberly jabbed her.

Blue barked happily, and everyone started to laugh.

Eleven

Will parked the truck next to the sprawling white farm-house, grumbling under his breath. He didn't know what was so urgent about checking out the house sitting on the new property the Sutherlands had recently purchased, but his father had been adamant that it be done immediately. Rather than argue a point Will had no hope of winning, he'd turned on his heel and stalked out of the room. The older Sutherland had done a fair job of keeping a cocky grin off his face, but Will had still scowled.

Trudging through the snow with the use of his cane, he wished his mother hadn't been humming a Christmas tune when she'd passed him on her way into her sunny kitchen from God-only-knows where. He didn't care if there were only six days until Christmas, it was downright rude of his parents to enjoy the season this year.

Cort claimed his brother was ornerier than a pet snake. Grasping the doorknob with one hand, Will had to agree with him. But then, Cort was pretty grumpy himself. Women troubles tended to have that effect on a man.

Will was so engrossed in his dark thoughts he didn't hear the first series of high-pitched barks. By the time the third set of yips reached his ears, his hand stilled on the door-knob.

What the—

For the first time, he noticed the wreath on the door. He stopped fishing for the key in his coat pocket and tried the knob. The door swung open on a discordant squeak.

Will had been inside the big country kitchen a couple of times when he was a kid, back when the Trentons had lived here. But nothing could have prepared him for what was awaiting him this afternoon.

"Hi, honey, you're home," Krista said breezily, as if seeing him standing in the gaping doorway of a house he was sure she'd never set foot in before was an everyday occurrence.

"Krista. What...how...who?"

"Unless you want to heat the entire state of Nebraska, you'd better close the door," she said, a mischievous gleam lighting her eyes.

Will must have closed the door, although he'd never be sure how he managed such a feat. Krista was standing on the third rung of a short stepladder, looking for all the world as if she was hanging blue-and-white gingham curtains. Her soft white sweater followed her curves, the oversize collar framing her face, the hem tucked into the waistband of a flowing red skirt.

"How was your day?" she called airily, lifting the curtain rod into place.

Her words barely registered on his dizzy senses. Feeling like an idiot, he took a deep breath, trying to clear his thoughts. Feeling slightly woozy, Will looked around. An undecorated Christmas tree was visible on the other side of a curved archway. Here in the kitchen, woven place mats were stacked on the edge of the counter. A coffeemaker sputtered as the last water drained through the filter and a freshly baked cinnamonny concoction was sitting on top of the stove. The place looked homey, inviting. What the hell was going on?

Before he could voice the question out loud, a potted daffodil rattled in its saucer. In the blink of an eye, Tommy ran into the room, his big-footed puppy close on his heels. "Oh, hi, Daddy, you're home."

Daddy?

Without conscious thought, Will's mind registered the significance of those two tiny words. *Daddy* and *home.*

"Well," Krista said, brushing her hands on her softly gathered red skirt and stepping down from the ladder. "What do you think?"

Will was having a little trouble with her question. Truth was, he couldn't think. But he could react, and he swore he'd never reacted so strongly to anyone in his entire thirty years.

"Your mom told me I could call her Grandma," Tommy declared, smiling for all he was worth. "Isn't that cool? I've never had a grandma before."

"You've met my mother." It was a statement, not a question, directed at Krista as much as at Tommy. Their subsequent nods were completely unnecessary; Will should have known his mother was up to something when she'd disappeared at the crack of dawn this morning.

He couldn't get enough of looking at them. Wisps of hair had escaped the loose style on top of Krista's head, fanning her face and neck. There were dark smudges beneath her eyes, making him wonder how long it had been since she'd slept. Despite her obvious fatigue, her eyes glowed with excitement, and a smile curved her lips so softly it took his breath away. Tommy was grinning, too, the little urchin, his eyes bespeaking a smugness way beyond his years.

"Your parents have been so helpful," Krista declared, walking ever closer. "Your dad started the furnace and carried in the Christmas tree and your mother helped me here in the kitchen. This house is incredible. It has seven bedrooms. Seven! But then, we're going to need a lot of bedrooms, don't you think? After all, Gina, Taylor and the triplets are going to visit every summer."

Her voice was growing softer with every word she spoke. "And I'm sure Tommy's going to want Stephanie to come along."

She stopped before him, little more than two feet away, her voice, by now, barely above a whisper. "Tommy can have his pick of rooms, and I've always wanted to have another baby or two. And Will? If you don't say something pretty soon, I'm sure I'm going to wither away to dust."

As he looked at Krista, every uncertainty Will had felt these past eight days evaporated into thin air. This was his Krista, a regal daffodil bravely pushing her way toward the sunshine, strong yet vulnerable in a way that stole into his heart, through his mind, all the way to his soul.

The past week had been hell without her. He'd wished a thousand times that she would have begged him to bring her with him to Nebraska. Instead, she'd shown up unexpectedly, her eyes glowing with a serene and steadfast inner peace. He'd been afraid to uproot Tommy. She seemed to have no such qualms. "What about that one-of-a-kind school?" he asked.

"I'd rather he had a one-of-a-kind father."

Her words soaked through his senses, filling him with good old male conceit, not to mention old-fashioned Suthrland smugness. "Only another baby or *two*?" he finally asked. "I was thinking more like an entire baseball team."

Krista's breath caught in her throat. Will looked more drawn than she'd ever seen him, and there was a crease lining one cheek she didn't remember, but she'd recognize that cocksure grin of his anywhere. He was accepting her arrival in Nebraska, into his life. Arms wide open, he was accepting *her*.

She went into his arms, tucking her face into his neck and wrapping her hands around his back as if she'd never let him go. "An entire team?" she asked, his last statement finally filtering through her entrancement. "Then we're going to have to get busy."

His cane clattered to the floor in his haste to mold her more tightly to his body. The puppy barked and Tommy giggled. Will kissed Krista's cheek, her temple, her chin.

She let her gaze roam over his face, across the dark stubble on his chin, touching upon his proud nose, his straight eyebrows, on up to his honey brown hair, slightly askew in the front, as always. Before her stood a man, a wonderful man, a man who wasn't perfect, but perfect enough, a man who loved her, and loved Tommy. How could she have ever doubted that?

She took both his hands in hers. Finally finding her voice, she said, "I know you love me. But would you say it. Just once?"

For the first time since his accident over five months ago, Will swept the woman he loved into his arms, lifting her off her feet and twirling her in a circle. "I love you, Krista. I love you, I love you, I love you. If you'll agree to marry me, I'm going to say it every day for the rest of our lives. I love you."

Blue barked, nipping at Will's pant legs. Giggling, Tommy leaned down to reprimand his dog, and Will lowered his mouth to Krista's. Their lips met like a promise, dreamy, intimate, more binding than any words could hope to be.

"I love you," Will whispered against her mouth.

"And I, you," she answered.

"Did you hear that?" Tommy called.

Will and Krista both listened. It came again, an almost magical sound of sleigh bells coming from far, far away.

Tommy ran to the window. Arms wrapped around each other's waist, Krista and Will followed. The sound of sleigh bells came a third time, tinkling through the twilight, yet there wasn't another soul in sight.

The new fallen snow cast a hush all across the countryside. The newly formed family standing in that window felt that hush inside their hearts. The sun was nearly gone, the western horizon a brilliant shade of pink, casting a glow for miles around.

"It's going to be a wonderful Christmas," Krista whispered to Will and Tommy.

"The best," Tommy declared, scampering off to play, cups rattling in their saucers in his wake.

Will turned Krista into his arms, fitting her close. "He called me Daddy," he said, his voice dipping low, adding to the magic of the snow-covered landscape and the miracle of the season.

Krista stood on tiptoe, brushing a lock of hair from Will's forehead. "I've never seen him so happy," she said softly.

"That's because all his Christmas wishes have come true," he said, that Sutherland smile lifting his lips in a way that took her breath away.

"It's a miracle," she whispered, drawing his face down to hers.

"A miracle," Will agreed a moment before his lips found hers in a kiss that was filled with dreamy intimacy and unspoken promises.

Somewhere in the old house a puppy barked and a little boy laughed. Lovers sighed, and words of love were whispered. It was truly a miracle, one that had only just begun.

*   *   *   *   *

COMING NEXT MONTH

#973 WOLFE WEDDING—Joan Hohl

Big Bad Wolfe

No one ever thought January's *Man of the Month,* Cameron Wolfe, was the marrying kind. But a romantic getaway with brainy beauty Sandra Bradley suddenly had the lone wolf thinking about a Wolfe wedding!

#974 MY HOUSE OR YOURS?—Lass Small

The last thing Josephine Morris wanted was to let her infuriating ex, Chad Wilkins, permanently back into her life. Yet when he proposed they have a wild, romantic *affair,* Jo just couldn't say no....

#975 LUCAS: THE LONER—Cindy Gerard

Sons and Lovers

Lucas Caldwell knew better than to trust the sultry reporter who suddenly appeared on his ranch. But Kelsey Gates wouldn't stop until she got her story—or her man!

#976 PEACHY'S PROPOSAL—Carole Buck

Wedding Belles

Peachy Keene just wasn't going to live her life as a virgin! So she proposed a no-strings affair with dashing Luke Devereaux—and got much more than she bargained for.

#977 COWBOY'S BRIDE—Barbara McMahon

Single dad Trace Longford would do anything to make new neighbor Kalli Bonotelli sell her ranch to him. But now the rugged cowboy not only wanted her ranch—he wanted Kalli, too!

#978 SURRENDER—Metsy Hingle

Aimee Lawrence had found Mr. Right—but he insisted she sign a prenuptial agreement! Now he had to prove his feelings for her ran much deeper than lust—or there would be *no* wedding....

INTRODUCING... **WINNER'S CIRCLE**

A collection of award-winning books by award-winning authors! From Harlequin and Silhouette.

Falling Angel
by Anne Stuart

WINNER OF THE RITA AWARD FOR BEST ROMANCE!

Falling Angel by Anne Stuart is a RITA Award winner, voted Best Romance. A truly wonderful story, *Falling Angel* will transport you into a world of hidden identities, second chances and the magic of falling in love.

"Ms. Stuart's talent shines like the brightest of stars, making it very obvious that her ultimate destiny is to be the next romance author at the top of the best-seller charts."
—*Affaire de Coeur*

A heartwarming story for the holidays. You won't want to miss award-winning *Falling Angel,* available this January wherever Harlequin and Silhouette books are sold.

Big Bad
WOLFE

THE WEDDING YOU'VE ALL BEEN WAITING FOR....

WOLFE WEDDING
by Joan Hohl

January's **Man of the Month**
and book 4 of the #1 bestselling Silhouette Desire
miniseries, **Big, Bad Wolfe.**

Known as "The Lone Wolfe," January's
Man of the Month, FBI agent Cameron Wolfe, is
hardly the marrying kind. But when an invitation to
his baby brother's wedding makes the other Wolfe
brothers line up at the altar, will Cameron also say
"I do"? Sandra Bradley sure hopes so—because there's
a little Wolfe on the way!

Don't miss *Wolfe Wedding* (it's full of happy
surprises!) by Joan Hohl, available this January,
only from

▼ SILHOUETTE®
Desire®

Coming in 1996 from

SILHOUETTE®

Desire®

SONS AND *Lovers*

A new series by three of romance's hottest authors

January—LUCAS: THE LONER by Cindy Gerard

February—REESE: THE UNTAMED by Susan Connell

March—RIDGE: THE AVENGER by Leanne Banks

SONS AND *Lovers* : Three brothers denied a father's name, but granted the gift of love from three special women.

"For the best mini-series of the decade, tune into SONS AND LOVERS, a magnificent trilogy created by three of romance's most gifted talents."
—Harriet Klausner
Affaire de Coeur

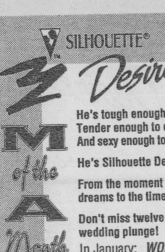